In the country of
the skin

By the same author

The Collector and Other Poems
  Routledge & Kegan Paul

The Nature of Cold Weather and Other Poems
  Routledge & Kegan Paul

At the White Monument and Other Poems
  Routledge & Kegan Paul

The Force and Other Poems
  Routledge & Kegan Paul

Dr Faust's Sea-Spiral Spirit and Other Poems
  Routledge & Kegan Paul

Work in Progress

In the country of the skin

Peter Redgrove

Routledge & Kegan Paul   London

Fiction
Redgrove, P
I5
1973

First published 1973
by Routledge & Kegan Paul Ltd
Broadway House, 68–74 Carter Lane,
London EC4V 5EL
Printed in Great Britain by
Western Printing Services Ltd,
Bristol

ISBN 0 7100 7514 6

PR6035
.E26
I5
1973+

For Penelope

Out at sea
Waves flee up the face of a far sea-rock, it is a pure white door
Flashing in the cliff-face opposite,
Great door, opening, closing, rumbling open, moonlike
Flying open on its close.

one

My skull is like an elaborate caisson, a confectioner's appari-
tion of cooked jellies. I carry cancellation behind me like a
spreading stain. There are no back-days. This is the way I invent them. In the sky I select a quiet space shaped like a bell.
I give it a push and it begins tolling. It fills up with iron. The
iron sheds round it grey church-stone. Your mother walks
through the studded doors wiping her thin warm spectacles.
We are happily married and your gold ring is tuned to an A.
The reception is at an inn with a courtyard where a squat
black fountain plays with itself incessantly.

The little salty pools shiver with relish, that has something
to talk about. Love says commandments with us to prove that
he is not and never has been a ghost. At the end of his recital
a thundercloud the size of Highgate breaches its walls, it is
full of silver light and another woman's voice. I wander
among them wondering what they talk about, the little silver
rock-pools singing and saying poems. The city is one great
lantern full of the voices of my friends. There is a drowsy
moon like a great pilchard-skin. The beach is a stone god with
the heart of a crab.

There is the cloth of a blouse running over its shoulder,
criss-cross, criss-cross, live dead, live dead. There is a large,
paunched room in white and gold. There is the electricity of
her fingers and the path opened for it by everyone. There is
she (there are too many of them) who smells of strawberries in
the fontal evening, and a silver vase for the red rose that (she
says) feeds on milk. But on the polished floor I did see, I think,

a churning platter of gold-and-crimson meat from which butterflies and locusts feed comradely, and their long shadows work like oars. There is a skylark and the sound of falling meteorites, and the song where at last her skin got to the white man and demanded payment.

Her reflections pace endlessly into the water. She is a girl on a bough until she is an old woman and her tears dip into the water. My tears' reflections on the faces of my sons come back to me through the water. She issues the water-passes, I need an ice-pass to the heart of the glacier, but she gives me a mineral-pass and I enter the water as a green stone. The great hollow, cupping the water, the green at the heart of it, and its reflections still clustering until the pond is full of black stones.

The forest binds its own jaws. Birds fold and fold and re-fold and unfold imaginary linens. There is a pattern of flies to this place like three cubes that fuse ten horizons, which is the spirit of the place seen edge-on. Its voice echoes: there are no funds. But there are funds. I sit tranquil by the dynamo with white muscles, the churching acre water-bed. It has funds.

This book has stolen the forest. I never open it now. I would open it for her, usually at page 300, prop it up on the baize of the card-table. After a minute or two, the wild sow would trot out, see us, and thunder across the green, stop non-plussed at the table-top, wheel and rush back into the book, which I held open at page 90. When the animal had disappeared I would clap the book shut and hold it close to her ear so she could hear the astonished clangour in chapter 9: the wild sow confounding the marriage of the baron's niece in the castle chapel. The acorns I shook from these chapters have made a carpet of oak-moss on the bookshelf; it is infested with tiny green snakes that talk. I am glad it is not a holy book, pillars of light would escape and glide about my house all night.

I am a man with a peeled stick and a whistle. A piece of red wax leaps out of my ear and becomes a red fox on the hill-side. My snot is a fat black toad. I keep him in a tobacco-tin and add to him. He rumbles in my overcoat. I have other

2

friends too slimy and deep to mention, and if you pick my flowers at night, if you steal from me, you will meet them. I have made a badger and a donkey from my hair and whiskers. When I pull the strings, the cattle low. On the hillside, among the foxes, a cloud passes through the bones of two animals that died fighting each other, and me.

The Magus relaxes. It being Shrove Tuesday and he the highest-ranking officer, he takes the throne. He hates the Practicus with the counter-tenor. There should be a mezzo-soprano for that part. It is time for his own work. He takes the athame, holding the hilt in his left hand, by the little finger.

A seagull cries on the wireless, its breath through the speaker smells of mussels, hers watching the blank fabric, of gas-mains. They embrace, his beak clanks on her buttons. Ghosts buzz in the broken bread. The oven coughs, she weeps, and lays her head back on its sill. Two childhoods fade as the door opens and the dog barks.

He asperses. He hands the athame to his counterpart. He lifts the rod from the table of manifestation by the female end.

No longer dead, the grass grows to music. I play the lush brown violin strokes. The forest springs up, swaying. Pizzicato gives me frogs dotting the marsh. Trombones pump daffodils into it. A roll of drums announces swallows. My baton drips with the one compendious note. I am conductor, though I did not write the piece. It is called Brief Afternoon on an A Flat Beach of Waves with a Girl the Colour of C Sharp Minor Who Knows the Score.

The veil wavers, and he is choosing cabbages. He smells their wet tissue and the earth at their foots. His glance falls to his shoes.

I hold the studio ballpoint. My study is furnished. My studio-couch brims with salt water at 70°. My typewriter is made of rushes. My potato clock chimes continuously, silently. My novel flows quietly from the spawn-tip of my frog-pen in black lines of yolk. Light pours from the yellow sun-sluice. They are coming to interview the black dolmen-stone tomorrow. Veins of warm humour branch through me. The novel flows from all of my pens. The frogs rest over my cool flanks. I am the world telling its story to itself. No scribbling thunder. Quietly telling, quietly telling.

He warms the crystal between his hands. He spat on it first, though that is not allowed. He let his name form in the crystal, Silas, then broke it like sugar into his other name, Jonas. He was rather surprised that Teresa was so helpful with this, though she didn't know it. Obviously she was on her heat, or hadn't bathed (which also was not allowed) and the furry dark smell helped him. He wanted to sleep with her, but this crumbled Jonas and Silas began to form again. He put the crystal down, and began to howl quietly, in Briah, and the crystal clouded, and crowded with knots, and cleared.

As I rush out, the splash of frosty dawn against me is a snowy ruffled shirt and a pair of nankeen trousers I had thought were buttercups. The sun rises. A red waistcoat now, and a green bow tie. I open my mouth to taste the sun with my sliver of blue sky. I shall stay here for my raven-tailed coat and my thistling hair of starlight.

The howling modulates AAAAEEEEEAAAA.

I hold out the frying-pan and wish. My breakfast drops into it. Two beautiful silver eggs with gold yolk. But I cannot eat replicas. I slam the safe door on another breakfast.

I nicked my finger on the sword! I see the blood-answerer loom down. The finger should go into the brazier now, but I can't. Teresa knows. She doesn't blame me. She's as weak as I am. I knew this was coming. The oak of the beams is boughs, they sway. The roof is a ship. I stand in the ship. I wish I knew more before I began. Somebody may help.

He lives: in the quality of saliva.

He lives: in breakfasts and the smell of clean towelling.

He lives: in one kind glance from the eyes of Queen Mary.

He lives: in a coil of laundromat washing, the snails are his recognised friends.

But he also lives: where the birds have well-developed

4

stings and the naked servant brushes up the dancing-
girls' limp disabled shadows.

II

The earthworm crosses the dark woodland path, starlit.
My hostess is a flower and a seamless egg.
She orders the plants to come and the spoons to serve me.
They scoop black roes. Stars shine where they scoop.
Tears slide from my finger-ends. Lakes vanish overnight.
I chew the herb that opens all locks. I pass famished, without
penalty.
I watch the rain burning my books.
A horse of mud reins out of the mists.
The clock is an orchard of wheels,
A carving that moves piecemeal through lunch,
And a little squandrance, downcast and overborne.
The brigade of guards presents arms in front of the frozen
waterfall,
The rooms in unison pronounce their bedtime prayers,
I request antler largoes of seaswell,
The computer-organ constructs an endless seashell made of
gunfire.

The butcher swells his slice-apron,
He sings his steel for me in the morning sunshine.
His sawdust buzzes with the blue retinues,
The blue sisterhood of the afternoon
And by the evening their fly-emperor
Strides into Frome, Faust in his pocket.
I see the small scared face stark on the blue buzzing serge.
Night accumulates in Somerset.
Among the blue-black there are light blue ghosts of cricketers
Frondy in the dark. Their game started
In the hot noon-day blood.
Their game went on in the evening bonfire.
A stick cracked; faint voices: 'Well-played, Sir!'

5

Meanwhile Grannie's lace abolishes itself.
She strangles. A cloud trails stealthily
Through the church, erasing the hymnbooks.
Who would hold yet another service? He will,
Despite the cowherd on the hill
Who whistles as he whittles crucifix after crucifix
For his flock. The sacred clerk
Tipples with bent head, he concentrates
On the iron bell, too heavy to toll,
On the green sun that will not explode,
On the leeches that have drunk the clock up.

The room was shaking with envy as I walked in, so I turned, spat on Tomas' carpet, and left, laughing. I didn't see why he should get any of my money, but meanwhile his envy was shivering me to pieces. Was I supposed to pay to quieten that? The world might very well be a bundle of fragments, it was Yeats' opinion when he was young, and he gave many lectures on the proposition. Occasionally he met an old man who agreed with him, and they had a very unified conversation. I wanted to stroke the old man, and I went to bed with him and fondled his silly crooked back and his little grapefruit tummy and his limp cock. He was not only an old man, he found me unattractive too. Anyway I was drunk, on vodka, so he wouldn't know.

This urn awaits, a cool cruet for a hot head. I put my ear to the ribbed chantry or well-core. One water-drop chimes. There is a violet cheese. A cool, taut bed. Grapes. As she plays, my candle ancestors appear in pouting wax. A rose opens. A firefly alights on the waxed buffet. Egg drips down her amethyst shirt. I raise the cleaver, but a sweet word deflects it. My ancestors applaud from the window, with bone music.

The barman with the frail silky whiskers said, I'm sorry, I like to be friendly with everyone when I'm tired, love keeps on coming, I hand out beer as fast as I can, they order so little, I want the large coloured advertisements to bring increasing cellarage and sweating blond barrels and more swag-bellied Sunday mornings into which I can give I can give with a smile, and a twitch of his frail silky whiskers as he drank a small glass of water into which he had poured from a folded paper a few grams of a silvery dust.

Jesus contemplating the wounds in his hand. His head a frail gold shell in the light-burst of the halo. A personage in the next window holding a cup of gold, and a small green serpent winding itself round the cup. Daffodils planted in every corner of the old stone, for Easter. Over the main altar, Jesus hanging by his wounds in a deep blue window, with eyes closed, as in a sea.

They have laid wardrobes of themselves aside on summerhouse windowsills; the horny spindles under the trees, the prickly chandeliers, in the last sunshine they have muted a complicated dust, a coherent ash, vacant body-masks, air-vases with eyed canopies and mandibles, sophisticated whiskers, their meddling nectar has boiled away, these sensitive waters donned these suits to die among us for a while. I watch her photo from the bed, the vacant papery reminder.

I nudged my puke with a forefinger through the grid of the drain, squeezing it through until it disappeared with a plop a few inches below. My throat still smarted with the ejected gin and sausages, but the chilly stone that hurt my knees loved me, and I enjoyed my craftsmanship.

Twilight sucks the lupins. Her diningroom table shines like a marshland. The airy mountaintops are spread with spotless linen. Her ghost has no heart and irons the towels. It is a shell-shaped space, she sets her hair in a shell-shape, I met her shadow with the long hair flowing, in the lane. It stood aside for me, sighing inconsolably.

Where the crucifix hung, there is a light crossroads on the dirty wallpaper. A faithful love hung there by its hands until it grew too ugly. Then it snapped the cross and stepped down. It is now one of the devils in hell.

Mary lowered her knitting. I turned back to my oiling, puzzled. Then I went and opened the window: the cows

7

were returning. Albert was at the gate, his hand on the latch, which looked like a Hebrew letter. Through the turf I saw the latched strata of rocks slowly lifting.

When she met him at the station his face was a mask of flame licking from the lips, like molten bronze dribbling from the hair, flickering round the eyes in their sockets like crucibles, running along each hair, and as he spoke the words made wings and splinters of flame like Chinese writing that loped across the platform at her; the furnace doors stood ajar on the blast. He had never been flame before, though he had often been a full jar of water silent and sweating softly in the shade, or a bronze gong that buzzed as she tapped it with cherry nails.

Under the thin gnat-singing of the filament, the font brimful with amber brandy. Gentlemen, the vicar said, let us eat and drink of Christ, and he belched. The doors shook and burst open. A long tongue of sunlight unrolled into the church and licked him up, burning. The earth shook in a tremendous purr. The ground cracked deeply into a chasm and the brandy flared briefly on its glowing sides. Whereas I, said the Colonel, I fare well. I hear the trumpet unfurling on the wind, the empty waterbottle by my bed fills tinkling to its brim; with a high thin singing from the millions of boulders grinding, the mountain bends, plucks a bough of blossom from the orchard and places it on my bedroom windowsill. Its warm perfume drifts in, for a moment I hear that white perfume play the snatch of a gavotte on bells, then a whirlwind forms, a slim whirlwind that marches up and down the ranks of apple trees which have that instant swiftly come to ripeness. It plucks them and fills itself with rosy apples, and like a dancing girl carrying fruit in her skirt, fruit on her head, comes twirling in through the pots and pans, piles the fruit deep and ready on the stairs. She sings, apple-colonel, retired.

A museum like a beautifully-polished mass-grave. Cards on the cases like thin white informers. Special exhibits: the flying elk with its bronze urn; the great-father ghost-shirt; a

8

pickled oak Californian steering-wheel dressed in a suit of Mr Nixon's clothes and holding a bundle of receipts. At the exit, a diorama called: Mrs Dante is also taking the trip and Jupiter the source of life is troubled.

I searched the encrusted walls. Long, transparent crystals, in the heart of each, a thing. An embryo-comma, man or horse; in another crystal, light blue, a marriage taking place. As I watched the bride's mother began wiping her thin spectacles with a spotless hankie, very slowly to begin with, then faster and faster until I had to look away. I wanted frameless windows I could step through. I scraped at these but cut my hand, I bled and this fed the scenes, the wedding went into a white and black flicker, then a grey blur as a drop of my blood touched it; a tear dashed from my eye struck an embryo crystal and with a loud tick the horse or man grew one size larger. Then another room like walking in between floating ponds full of their reflections, ruffling a little as I passed. A dog in a hedge peered up with a bristling look. Next door I saw a woman attacked by a hurricane: she had caught one brick with a hand above her head, but only one out of a swarm that were attacking her, visible death. Her fist glowed white on the red stone, poor dead lady. In her velvet head was such a seated sweetness, her smile in all this had no trace of grimness. Then I saw her strain and reverse, and throw the brick back and all the other bricks fluttered after it and built the town up again, the clock tower came to rest under its canopy, and the church bells began chiming, and she turned to me and smiled and said, I did it for you, you know. I began to pick at the crusty scab on my hand-wounds. I turned away, ashamed, wishing she had not built the same life up again, just as it was before.

When the police knocked on the door and shoved in we were all so high we laughed all the way to the station and laughed at the magistrate in the morning. I laughed and I lost everything, it wasn't the first time. My wife left with the children, there was a big fine and the maintenance. I still laughed all the time, and keep on laughing.

9

A drop of water fell on my forehead. I was the Emperor of Abyssinia, and the plumes waved in my crown. Silas tickled my nose. I was a creeper growing sideways in the forest and I supported forty clumps of berries with great joy. Silas rubbed eau-de-cologne on the back of my hand. I was in a ballroom with other officers of the guard, in my arms a white muslin lady. Silas struck the table with a fork. I was thigh deep in mud. On the bank in front of me many alligators in unison opened their maws. A foul wind blew. Silas shone a torch at my forehead. It made me Suleiman. Shone it at the back of my neck. My shirt opened deeply in la toilette de guillotine. He brought a hot iron near my face. I was up early to greet the sun, and drew the curtains to hear the birds more clearly. Behind me Teresa pleaded for me to come back to bed. Then Silas cut my jugular vein. My head swam the river, singing as the sky grew dark. The water dried to a silver web, my head caught like a fly. Teresa came loping along though she wore a terrible spider mask and picked my head up like a crumb of bread. She placed it in Silas' lap. Here he is, Silas. I wept with gratitude. He fastened me to the chain around his neck. He put me to his ear and I whispered praises.

Silas and Teresa, in a peaceful time, began living together. Their cottage was on a headland, a good place, where the waves all split in two before their prow of rock, where the currents revolved in figures-of-eight which were dangerous for bathing. Silas said that they therefore reminded him of infinity on two counts. The name of the cottage was Sheerfin. For both of them this was a good name, a name that did not inspect them, one that sometimes whistled on two notes down a dewy corridor. Lying in the bedroom overlooking the sea, inside each other, differentiation of sex vanishing in Karezza, they both knew how to change the house, alter the weather, but they preferred to enter the alchemy of the old stones instead, imposing nothing. Each stone was a receiver and a transmitter. Its history could be read with the palm of a hand, though one must keep awake: Silas found Teresa in a trance and she seemed to have sunk into the stone up to her elbow.

She was back to the forest mud, before the stone was formed, and partly in the butterfly and partly in the flower it pollinated. Silas warned her to wear her rings on both hands, she now had no choice but to be what she was, and the rings were safeguards, like snow-shoes and guide-dogs. She took his rebuke with pleasure and irony, and lay down in the passage with her legs open. They were a cavalry of lava, which slowly set. The cottage distilled them, it distilled them upstairs to bed with the coloured dream-images surging around their heads, it distilled them downstairs after the night of glass cameras and transparent bird-cages and tunnels underneath the world. One afternoon as she was dressing for tea, winding a white rosary about her neck and collar, a tall sandy-haired man peered over her shoulder in the mirror. The room was empty. She wanted approval from him, but she also wanted to ask angrily, what is this old man doing in our house? And also, what right have we? And what can I do to help? And despite my ghost-skill, which is absent-minded at the best of times, I am frightened. Just for a moment the stone caught her again and water rose in the walls and bounded over the bookshelves, and faces gaped at her from the torrent. One sandy-whiskered face pulled itself out of the stream and limped over to a small shed that she now saw was in the garden, which she was watching from the bedroom window. Silas called from downstairs, she must have been there for a considerable time. She told him of her encounter with the ghost. He looked at her and said, that is the man I put in my pendant. That door must lead into this stone. We must on no account enter. But they spent a happy hour over tea making jokes about fugitives escaping up their own back passages. They were both glad that the sandy-man had learnt enough to get out and about, and even lay traps for them!

But he's weak, very weak, Silas said. Listen to the way he began. He laid his neck stone on the table. It spoke.

I love God and I smile to myself. I have prepared a tablet that will survive mud, earthquake, gravel, because of the plaintive wisdom that is written on it. This wisdom has efficacy because in a tight spot it moves the tablet on, with the hand of whoever is holding it. It reads: 'Seek simplicity. Distrust it.' He offered me a glass of sherry in his pale blue living room, and there the wine looked like transparent teak. He lifted his glass, his moustache was a shade darker. He said, seek simplicity. Distrust it. I thought, be damned to his cheek offering me advice and said, just a minute, I must write that down. He said again, Seek simplicity. Distrust it. And dabbed his moustache with a handkerchief. I must have that handkerchief, I thought. I got it before I left. So with the vicar. I repeated the phrase to him after Sunday service. He frilled his lips with the expression that tells me the Church of England have vaults packed with bees and honey, golden sweetness, gold hair singing with energy and the whetting of their stings. A militant sweetness about his lips, he said: written on a tablet that would survive mud, wind, earthquake and gravel, for it is plaintive wisdom. I deal in plaintive wisdom, and know how it survives. But I caught the vicar's breath in my own new unused handkerchief. And I wrapped these two handkerchiefs into the heart of a wedge of clay which I fired into a new brick. And I wrote on the brick, Seek simplicity. Distrust it. Their silly mouths travel in the night-time. Something in his mouth wakes my elegant designer in his pink bedroom. It is the thorny stem of a rose. The vicar runs from his bed in a panic, spitting out molasses.

III

A glow-worm in the sea-night, the comfortable cottage-rooms lighted brilliantly in each segment with lamps burning insect-oil. From its head the stag-beetle mounts guard over its shuttered rooms with strong spread-toothed tusks. The elephant comports its strong-rooms on spreading columns. The dragonfly is primed with whirring mechanisms of cellophane. The badger is locked up by a solicitor until the debentures are found. But the thing that pilots the bluebottle was once seen by the Rabbi of Prague after prolonged fasting. He ordered the exile psalm sung three times over, and his attic closed. The sun has nothing to hide; the moon is a door left swinging by the personage who has passed through: my eye is a long road to an imagined city, which is rich as white paper.

Rich as Teresa's white blouse, still going criss-cross, criss-cross. She smiles, and lies down on the bed. She looks down and frowns as she undoes one button, turns her head and smiles again. He slides his hand through the opening, finds no bra, an incredible softness.

It is as if someone constantly swung the handle and changed the plots. It is as if the whole peninsular swung on hinges and clicked into a new setting. It is as though the rocks became radium and the air became crackling nylon. I can feel your personality in your handclasp, it is boiling silver in the grip of your fingers. Your hair leaves streaks in the air. We ease into the green weed now. It twists its precipices round us and fresh human wreckage hoves into sight. Someone's head pokes round that door a hundred years ago and his eyes under sandy hair meet mine. Then the house heaves and we sit in the middle of a summer-house woven of twigs on a dusty wooden floor. It is made of a basketwork of birdcries. Then I am in a fresh shift and the doors are all water-doors and sluices and the canals are disused and the gates are slimy. I go into the house and the fish shines in the larder like Orion just appearing in the sky. There is a cold grate of blue clinker and a plate of cold chicken. Then at other times we are fully human, and we kiss.

Silas had noticed the clock when he first started thinking about his headache like coloured liquids and confectionery under pressure in his skull, and he heard the bottom stair chirrup as Teresa started to come up. It took her fully ten minutes to decide to come to bed. A little bit of a tease. Mostly a sincere desire for his comfort.

The clock is like a greenhouse. Within glass walls, plantations of springs and cogs all moving slightly in jerks. The clock is like a bedstead. Time rapes his mistress and the mattress chimes. In the undertaker's parlour, my great uncle,

13

hands clasped across his chest, conceals the wound where the doctor pierced his heart. The old ticker must not beat underground. On the undertaker's parlour's mantelshelf, the electric clock buzzes. The electric clock is full of bluebottles, in honour of my great-uncle. She fills the water clock like a greenhouse with horseleeches. Egg drips down her amethyst shirt. She has broken the ticking hen clock. A soft word deflects the sabre. The war clock misses a beat. He draws a resounding chord from the orchestra clock, which has to complete the sixth symphony by eight twenty-nine exactly. Many of these I observed in the television screen, which though both handless and square, is filled with works, and disposes of time in dismembered portions, which grow stale easily.

And Silas must do his magic, and be called Jonas; and Teresa does her magic because she loves Silas, but not Jonas; and she instructs Silas without knowing it; and Silas discovers Jonas with his magic; and Jonas does not love Teresa, and she knows it.

The birds above the roofs weaving their solid savours through the air catch the involved note in his voice, the knot in his words, the knot in his flesh, the knot in the meat, and they ramify externally, as if they were not meat. As he feeds them he cries TALUS to each one, they return into the air crying TALUS, TALUS between their beaks, muting white TALUS and the air is full of the rolling shingle of talus-shouts and this is the past and now a child is sitting on the lawn with an old man, and they are studying a book of life and the child cannot understand the message of the book because the air is full of the jostling talus-shouts of dead bird-flocks and the tiny echoes of talus left in the voices of progeny that nip and hop in the garden now. And the child is weeping because he can't understand the book whose words say only talus, talus, and the old man is weeping because his work is weeping because it cannot understand and cure the child of talus, which is a stone put in his head from the idle death-cry of a magician in that garden eleven years ago, it was his mantra and the child hear-

14

ing it as he died had to take it, no one else would. In dreams the dark head of the child flies with the silver one of the old psychiatrist and their eyes brim with electricity and their teeth flash in the talus-cry.

Teresa's darkness is still infested with winter vampires. They get into the house and they get into the daylight and they almost get into the sunlight but not quite. This is what they look like, she says to Silas, who puts on his Jonas look and says, tell me carefully. A steak-knife and a meat-hammer. A nail on a plate. A patch of marram-grass with blood on the tufts; it has been cutting somebody to the bone who tried to snatch it. A night-cramp that pulls the fingers away from the light-switch. A glass of stale water by the bed with the humped shape in it: its walls are filmed with algae. Boughs piled in the winter woodshed like a collapsed and bearded spider. A cathedral in the dusk full of red fire. A rusty knife in fresh red meat. A lettuce-leaf caught under a scraping door. Sand blowing under the door of the bedroom all night, heaped up in udder shapes. The slippery model of a tooth the size of a sentry-box. I peer into its cavities that smell like an opened sepulchre. Liquid splashes out onto my skirt and a microbe wriggles like a chocolate eclair in the saucer-shaped caries. Silas looked like Jonas again: it is one demon, he said. Think of it as one demon, and give it a name. I almost get a name, but I can only see a plate of slices of raw beef. Step into the middle of this plate, says Jonas, you are the size of a salt-cellar. Kick off your shoes first, the meat is bloody, get blood on your stockings. Oh Silas, the meat is curling up at the edges and calling out to me, it twists itself into a stomach. Jonas replies, don't keep it off, if you do it'll digest you, pull it to you. I do, it's digested my clothes I can feel it against my skin and my skin tastes raw beef tingling like horseradish. Your body must swallow it, tasting it. It's me! cries Teresa, it is the meat under my skin, I can feel my skin! Jonas turns his head away, and Silas comes into view again, looking pleased.

Shall I tell you my water-graduation exercise, he asked.

There is the mist which runs up a provisional monastery of grey aisles and churning alleys; there is the broken bridge like the skeleton of a stork (a bad mark for that, since it is not water, and I made several more mistakes): there is a milestone and then a milestone and then a milestone towards the sea and then there is a field of grey milestones made of mist and a church made of mist (my examiners were pleased that I had recovered myself after those stones). The mist completes and reconstructs with reverent emotions tonight, annexes of this seed-church along the mountains; this mist still echoes with the shot with which the drunken farmer killed his sheepdog, and that was many nights ago; there is the sea, and the shot echoes through the scaffoldings of the mist abbeys built over the whole sea as far as France, and grey monks walk the waves; and far out below the waves there is the one particular mussel I choose who, having constructed the two halves of his church of purple chalk filtered from the whole ocean, reclines glutinously and in the perfect darkness which by the pressures of the water on his soft body is perfect vision to him, pricks out and begins to build a moon of pearl on its inner surface. It is hermaphrodite, but they quarrel over the shape of the moon, and Venus rises from their shell, leaving Hermes sleeping exhausted hidden in its depths, and she steps ashore again as she always did. I got marks for moving earth into and out of water as dissolved calcium carbonate, and for introducing a pearl, which is reputed to be fire resting in water, and for making my magus-creature bisexual. My water-mists moved in air as well, and had I left the dead bird-bridge out and had a more emphatic fire somewhere on the waves, I might have made the inner temple with my four elements and my two sexes. But did you have to make all this happen, asks Teresa. Oh no, said Silas, I had to make a cardboard sigil with all the appropriate rites, and it didn't matter that nobody supervised me, because when the examiner pressed the disc to his forehead he was supposed to see all that I had put into it. And he did. He told me everything I wanted to happen. He was a great man. And a good one, for once. He was called Tomas.

I met him when I was a boy. I had something wrong with my nerves in those days because I would hear all the birds shouting the word talus, which is geology for dry shingle or scree. Sometimes when I was reading all the books were written in just this one word. Tomas came to try and cure me, but I don't think he was much good then, because one day he just sat on the grass with me crying, and that was the last I saw of him until my examination. I used to think he was so holy he had become a box of a man with several lights in it arranged in rows and looking steadily at each other. These lights would be flashing colours, and of rapidly alternating sex, or a new sex. This gave me an odd little boy's sex feeling, which was linked with getting caught in the rain, or rolling in mud. Once I rushed out into a thunderstorm in my grey school uniform and masturbated rolling on the lawn in the rain – it was lovely. Sometimes still as the sun comes out I notice there are benches in me with people sitting on them looking at each other, and the sunbeams dance with motes that are arranged in rows. I can feel certain of Tomas' ideas in my breastbone as the sun comes up.

IV

They are not sheep on these hills, they are rain-bringers. They are thunder, lightning, and the like. The name of the flock is Silas. One of its names. I will tell you the other one soon. How the thunder bangs! Look up above – there is the mask of God still bellowing and drifting slightly. Who is that in the shrubbery, in a wet evening gown? I know one of her names. Teresa arrived recently. I notice the bees are swarming by night, iced white by the moon. The name of the swarm is Jonas, or one of its names. My job is to polish the sweet jars in the attic that at the moment swings about the neck of Mr God Almighty Silas. One of my jobs. The low broad room of stone lined with dusty bottles. There are motes in the late sun dancing like voices all saying their names, which are Teresa also, and one other, which I am forbidden to tell you as yet, until you have changed into dry clothes. The stars are bony tonight, and the river bright like a kaolin worm: it is never the same worm twice so there is no point in telling you its name. Our hens are laying soft-skinned eggs now, for the stars take all their calcium, despite our prayers. There is also a granular stench in the refectory, and I fear scab hardens somewhere, like precious stones perfecting themselves in the earth, chalcedony or bezel, and the great gate rots on its posts. Moths called the sandy-haired man flutter against the putty-less panes rattling in the tall windows, the chanting of words called Sex, or Art, or it may be Magic, or Death, seeps through the rebuilt stables, and the horses that are there for the riding are called Kindness, Gaiety, Intuition and Poetry.

I can make him afraid, says Teresa to herself. I can haunt him with erosion, with darkness falling out of every pebble. He begins to fear the pebble and its outpourings, he fears the blood of the nearby hills, the outpourings of the rock. I will make endless soil and ponderous thick earth to wander through, I will preside from my hills, reflecting myself from my wet estuaries. I will go for walks with him in the woods that line the silted-up backwaters, and I will suddenly break free from his arm, and I will jump down into the purple mud, and I will lie at ease on it, an odalisque, among my cushions. I recline at ease in emerald flanks and winding satin clefts, he will find me in the places where clean ladies don't go, my finger up his anus, he wakes to find my finger there, he looks out of the window and he sees me playing with the broken egg-shells and cabbage stalks of the garbage, I see him, I wave and smile and smear tea-leaves down my skirt. I shin down cliffs of mud, I wade the estuaries, my skirt hitched up and my legs sleek, I wander through myself, mire gloats everywhere. Except that I could not do that to him, not bind him. Jonas already suspects that I could, Jonas knows how I could. That's why Jonas insists on the ritual baths; Silas knows that the furry woman-smell helps. Mire gloats. The lurching packs of birds bear mire-stings in their tails, they eat the fruit I grow and make more mud. He

18

admires the clean acid scut-bite of the fruit-bloated wasp. I
was rock, now I am endlessly deep and too soft for thought;
I am too much dark and power to stifle in. My rocks rot in
the clear rain. Sometimes he sees the clouds above the
shored-up mud tugged open as if by the hymns of mud
mud sings, my hymns to the sky out of my low dank softness.
Each night I skim out from hedgerows like huge glossy
slugs, hour-long transparencies with mire-cud inset deep, that
melts to glassy flesh that melts to mire. I am those hills that
spend themselves completely, leave place slowly in their
thick green dresses to bathe their heads and sink in ever-
mud.

Silas abandoned himself to mud-thoughts, though he believed it was not very good for his magic. He had thought that
when he was given the new name, Jonas, it was because he
had changed. Now he believes that the name is for a part
that was splitting off. In which case the outlook is not good.
He would have to go back to where the split had happened,
and choose a new path. Meanwhile he thought of the dirty
lady, and said he would keep his hands away from his penis.
That very dirty lady allows herself on certain occasions to be
picked clean by the flies, her numerous friends. They busy
themselves about her, they hum high – I am carrying earth in
my rostrum, for her! for her! Midges, even, with their soft
mouthparts are glad to manage a grain, a strand of mucus, a
thread of waterweed popping with animalculae. The big
blowfly bluebottle gobbles it off, crawling pugnose; her
streaming mud stripped off under the swarming particles
winking with wings like a blue sequined long-skirted dress;
then she steps forward out of this ink-cloud as radiantly
white as when she first stepped into the great mud. They
come when and as she needs them, mistress of flesh-flies, and
when she's dirty she can be clean as soon as she pleases, and
when she's clean she doesn't have to be afraid of being dirty.
How she likes being dirty! And now they clean her again as
she was before, laundered dry with the tiny breeze, the tight-
fitting weather of the fanning wings, and her white silk rustles

again. She walks on in that dense silk dress while the dirt is flown away behind her back until it is needed again. And on gold-veined wings, brass and fleshy blue pinions, by small brawny flies, frail grass-green ones, puffy and shiny-bun flies, the earth is carefully replaced, grain for grain, water-pattern for water-pattern, in the place where she wallowing took it upon herself. She has armies of flies in attendance, awaiting her pleasure, crouching low down behind her on knotty knees, these trains of priests in jointed horny vestments. When she moves on they follow behind in her track, under the leaves, through the tall grass in a low-walking river, like a black snake following behind watchful and winking with scales as she walks white-clothed through the green pastures towards the shrug-mudded river. They are a mixture of bird and greyhound. She may let the earth-dirt be for day upon day of progress and then the creases of her garments and her mud-caked hair will grow the small green things, stubble and fringes of green small beards of moss and green tresses. Now she is a green lady smelling of grass and ivy and there are bees and earthworms and Silas' hands fly to his trousers and begin rubbing hard and Jonas sings out that he sees the earthiness borne away in a glittering glass-and-wire cloud between the jaws of innumerable transparent flies, the sun effervescing their industry, the snot-coloured, polio-whiskered flies: they sing so sweetly that I cannot remember it, the wings of the guardian angels are velvet and black-fringed, my sins are seen very black, which is to say not seen, and then he's tarred and feathered and he comes in a sharp submissive spasm and Jonas feels sad.

v

But I detest birds, because they cannot kiss. Somehow I had summoned a grave presence of great strength and truth. Dressed in a shift she went to the cupboard and brought out bright cheese. The great table was scrubbed white, and first we ate. Then we loved, where she spread the great white

20

bolsters. She scattered crumbs for the birds. Returning her kindness those birds ate her plums. Grave presence, in that shift among the fruit trees. Great strength and truth treading with bare feet among the waspish cavernous plums. She was cavernous, but not waspish. She and the soft earth swarmed with liquors that felt. Among the trees hanging with ripe fruit, leaf-caverns bloomed and squeezed. The earth was wool-soft between the ancient boulders. Once it was raining and I came up to the garden gate and by the sundial saw an old woman or was it a young one I couldn't tell, until the life of the rain had drenched her to the young skin where the white shift clung. When I first came over the hill, that first night, I had walked too far, I knew nobody, but I had this address, the wife of a former friend. I thought it was the sea, but it was the blue-grey slate roofs gleaming in the hollow. I knocked at the door, she was much smaller than I had expected, she had big hips and an impudent grin, long dark hair, a white shift. She said come in and poured me a glass of straw-coloured wine. There was a big hearth with a fire burning on it, and the smell of timber and stone, like a well. There was a big white wood table, and a recess piled with bolsters and eiderdowns. I was in that house for twelve weeks. Nobody else came. On one side I remember that I was there, and I can still taste the wine and feel the shape of the glass I drank out of that first night. On the other side of things I cannot remember more than the edge of what we did, and I think she told me something I can't get out of my head. She said, I can see this morning you took up a black thread – look! I give you the white, look at me in my shift and take up the white strain. See me in the wet orchard in my shift and you will want me in the black earth, on the soft flower bed with the smell of the soil. She stood in white at the end of the orchard walk and she laughed as she tumbled in the soil and the earth streaked her cheek as she brushed her hair back. She stood at the end of the orchard walk in white like a soft waterfall with caves chuckling. Then I remember that the warm weather came with stubbles of green over the black and we spent days walking over warm turf. I have a picture of a blue flower knocking against a grey stone and the taste of a stalk of grass in my teeth, the turf warm and springy against the length of my body, and her voice saying, no more of this idolatry, do you hear?

VI

The town lights come on by the quays. The docks are one great ship floating high in the water next to the castle-hill. She still paints the nursery door like crooning. She paints it like crooning a terrible lullaby about maiden-death. She paints it blue in thick soft strokes like crooning. It is time to leave. First of all he says, I am ill. When that doesn't work, he goes back to bed. She continues painting, or crooning, it is all the same to him. He lies in bed and the winged head eases itself free, wriggles to and fro gently and there's a slight snap and the winged head flies out of the just-open window through the thistles of starlight. She has finished painting, and now she is in the kitchen crooning among the glimmer of red coals. The winged head sees the red window-frame, he picks it out from high above the castle, and he wishes they could love each other, there is so much landscape in that hate. Now he invents his own lullaby, about the girl who is the little flower that blooms only when the mind is blowing. Now he has mud-feelings, and thinks about the chain-letter that started him on his magic.

The chain-letter arrived by last post. It fell through the letter-box in its expensive thick envelope like a slice of white bread. I opened it, there was the sound of a trumpet blowing, it was written in violet ink. It told me to make three copies of itself and send them anonymously to three people who were good friends, or considerable enemies. It threatened misfortunes if I didn't do this, promised me good luck if I did. She was crooning with terrible paint-strokes and preparing to leave me, I knew, so my nerves were in no condition to resist the rite.

22

The letter said that I must dig into the multi-coloured clay, and the compass would help me. It told me how to make the compass: with a dish of rose porcelain and a golden needle floating on fresh milk. I had a goldplated tie-pin an aunt gave me when I was a schoolboy, and there was a thin porcelain cup in the local antique shop, so thin that the light shone through it in a delicate flesh colour. The gold needle had to be fastened to beechwood with steel bands. I used half a carpenter's pencil and a staple-gun. Then I was supposed to put these items by my bed and wait for further instructions.

That night I dreamed that a dark-haired woman in a white blouse and black skirt came into the pottery studio. She looked round and saw the long wooden chest by the furnace. She glided over to it, stepped in, lay down, sighed and wriggled. I walked over and looked down at her, her eyes were wide open, and the right lid came down in an enormous slow wink.

So I started to cover her with coloured clay slip from the dishes on the table, dashing it across her body from the small flat dishes. Her eyes flinched as I splashed her, then opened again, opening again her face where the clay had momentarily sealed it. First blue, then yellow, black, green and then red. Still her eyes cleared themselves from the clay. Then I took handfuls of red terracotta and packed the chest until it was level. Then I let the sides down. I had a coffin-sized wedge of clay with the girl inside, and I heard a whispering, and saw clay everting itself like a worm-cast, and I brushed the worm-cast off. There were two deep wells in the head of the wedge, I looked into them and saw dark water of eyes deep down within. Abruptly I swung open the furnace doors and rolled the slab inside. I closed the door and turned the switch to convert the slab to rock. As I turned away, I heard a thin whistling and I thought it was steam driving out of the twin wells, but then it seemed to come from outside the front door, and it was a faint ringing sound. I opened that door and there was the cup, the rose-coloured bowl, ringing under the blows of the rain. I looked down at myself and saw that I was

23

splashed with red like a butcher. Then I woke and found that pollen had slipped out of me as I slept. My mind held the image of the quarry of multi-coloured clay a few miles away. The dream meant I was to dig there, with the aid of the compass.

When I got to the quarry I took the compass out, unsealed a bottle of milk, and filled the bowl. I was surprised to find that the apparatus started to ring as I set the needle in it, just as it had to the falling rain in my dream. The needle swung, and I followed.

I was led to a face of red clay. As I came up to the cliff, the needle continued to point straight ahead into the clay, but the bowl stopped ringing, and lay hushed in the palm of my hand. I put it down, and noticed the powerful hose that was used to gouge out clay lying near by. I heaved on the spigot and began with living water to dig into the cliff, taking care not to undercut too much or it would fall on me and bury me alive. Shortly I had made a glistening crimson cavern, and as I played the hose around in the material, I saw a round shape streaming with clay blood emerge. It was a large boulder of quartz. I cleaned it with the water and turned the hose off. Nearly above my boots in the swamp-stuff, I clumped across to it, taking the compass that I had put on a ledge for safety. I held the compass directly above the boulder and the needle spun round and round; the ringing rose to a shriek until with a crack the bowl broke, splashing white milk over the crown of the red-streaked rock.

After that, events worked out right for me. The stone, about my own head-size, went into the disused grate of my very private bedroom. Shining a light into the stone showed me my magical name, Jonas. Thin cobweb veils running through the quartz spelt it out to me. I was always dreaming about women now, in dreams always changing the beds, spreading sheets of green, pink, crimson, yellow and black on wide high beds. I even met the girl of my dream! On our way back from the party she said she felt sick and wanted to go down to the river. We both fell in the mud, which was black in the moonlight, but at home, red under the shower. It was a good excuse to take our clothes off, but she left the next morning and I haven't seen her since, almost forgot her till now. I have my rock, my magic crystal and my new name, which burns so hard in my head sometimes I wish it would bite its way out of the blood-spotting quartz.

So saying, the wandering winged head full of musical crystals slips back into bed as the first light touches the sky with acid. The dawn looks like a beautifully-tuned piano made entirely of sea-shells. It goes ping-a-tunk with acrid notes as the mother o' pearl keys strike. At the aperture, window or larder or painting, wreathed with true lovers' knots and other cats-cradles my ancestors appear again. They are not memories, and I never dream, says Silas. However, this is what I see going on between the toast and marmalade and its shadow. So can I, says Teresa. She looks oddly crumpled as she plays, and there is a fly walking over her eye; the ancestors look as though they've been pulled out of chest o'drawers. But still, says Silas, there they go, with eyebrows raised and teeth glaring like relish and discoveries, the whole sad procession scrapes and rustles through the dumb-waiter to the sound of the mother o'pearl piano covered with papery photographs. We have had enough of them, says Teresa, I will pay her amply with tissuey money and forget all about her piano. Yes, let's go, says Silas.

Outside in the cold street that tune of hers had opened the tightly-wadded ancestor-files, alas. The clouds filled up with inherited faces and Silas and Teresa began conversing intently about the day's shopping. The spectacle won and the faces above with their horny teeth and floury gums tore themselves gently into bits that descended fluttering on the street and lined the boughs with white. Look, says Teresa, I am covered with my grandfather's white aunts. Well, says Silas, looking like Jonas, God has unleashed his archives and perhaps we can learn something. The pages shrivel on their palms as they bend to read. What did they come for? They met people coming towards them through the snow to the station, and these people were hunched so low by the weather they looked decapitated. But Teresa and Silas, though not Jonas, walked letting the watery white pages melt against their open eyes. Once they saw a pair of lovers running to the train laughing up into the sky, but when they looked into the faces they saw lantern-ghosts, flame-shadows playing on paper countenances, desperate flames sucking on low wicks. Then are we in love, ask Teresa and Silas of each other. She picked up snow from the wall and wedged it and rolled it into a snowball, threatened him, then looked more closely into it, holding it up in front of her face. It is million upon million of layered micropages for the compiling of preoccupied snowmen who allow black eye-holes to be punched into them with bits of coal. They are grateful to the spring and the sun for wasting all their conjecture and burning these pages into simple wriggling water. A white pain with coal eyes, a broomstick and an old hat for a cranium. And yet the flakes themselves are so silvery, like a chord, or the first word of our meeting. Greed kills then, he thought. Above all I am greedy. And she thought, above all I am greedy.

VII

It's Sarah now, the old woman beyond sex, the seventy-year-old who had the stroke, who wears a surgical boot, whose progress has the rhythm hop-scrape, hop-scrape, who tries to make life jolly sometimes with an air sadder than any mourning, her hair white, big busty woman, slowed down in jerks like dying film, Teresa's mother. Now she loves Jonas even if nobody else does, and can listen to Silas prosing on for hours and hours. They had dinner and were drinking coffee. Teresa and Silas took no alcohol as befits Magi with their own restraints and their own dissipations. Sarah, naturally, took a little orange curaçao. The evening was getting into a tight corner. But then Jonas appeared and Sarah relaxed because she recognised him from old, thought of him as twice-born, a man of her own age. Teresa said, I'm going to do the washing-up, but she went for a walk along the gusty edge of the common instead and watched the lights in the valley of pleasure-boats returning along the river. A little rain fell but that pleased her since she loved the sky to come on her skin, it made pictures and an excitement in her and a little star of wet on her knickers which was the water in her answering God's water.

Sarah was quite comfortable, and so was Jonas. With this couple it was sexual too, though the only genitals used were the voice and the ear. It was Sarah who, by caressing Jonas' word-penis, helped it grow. Western magicians offered a prize of a thousand pounds to anybody who could repeat the Indian rope trick. A fakir entered the compound accompanied by a little boy and a straw basket. Out of the basket he took a sabre and a coil of rope. He threw the rope up into the air and it stayed up, hooked to invisibility. He urged the little boy forward, but he hung back. With an angry gesture the fakir pushed him towards the rope. The little boy swarmed up it and as he got to the top slipped through some trapdoor in the air and winked out. The fakir was angry. Taking his sabre between his teeth he swarmed up the rope, but he did not disappear. He hung plainly visible, swishing the blade about in the empty air. With heartrending cries little pieces of boy and gouts of blood were cut out of nothing, fell spattering the audience and the sandy compound. The fakir looked down at what he had done, descended the rope slowly, tears streaming from his eyes. He picked up the pieces in a cloth, scooping up the bloodstained sand, wrapping the cloth round, putting it in the basket. His mood changed, he smiled, unthreaded the rope from the sky, laughed, tossed it in the basket, squatted down and began chanting and waving passes over the basket. A sensation like thunder in the air gathered around us in the compound and our ears popped. The lid of the basket came off and the little boy sprung up spitting out sand. He and the fakir bowed to the wildly applauding audience. My friend the Colonel, Sarah's dead husband, the grower of apples, apple-colonel retired, turned to me and said, what are they

27

clapping for? I recalled that he didn't speak the dialect.

Sarah did speak the dialect. She saw the Indian rope-trick. She could see all Jonas' effects, conjuring, visions and apparitions of all kinds, as he wished them to be seen, and possibly a little further than that, just to stretch him out, unlike the stately examiner Tomas. Tonight he discussed chess, and they talked together about the materials chessmen might be made of and how the game could be played. Pocket-sets; pocket-sets with radio for playing absent opponents; pocket-sets with radio and computer for winning; robot mansion-sets for playing on chequered patios (controlled by a handset, lurching and rumbling, disappearing through trapdoors when taken); Mardi Gras papier-maché sets: castles full of people with dark faces and bright clothes drinking up the festival, thirty-foot high naked queens manoeuvred by the girls' school, and black knights on white horses moved about by hard-shrieking boys. There was strip chess, and three-dimensional strip chess for older people, then the chess-men of maggots and worms, frozen by hypnotism like Moses' staff.

The chess-board strewn with rose-and-green maggots, the ivory pieces no longer ivory, but collapsing and looping maggots, caterpillars, worms that used to be pinched into chessmen shapes; now they leave the slashing moves for their own sinuosities. The exhausted players at the end of their tethers see a new game beginning. What could have caused life to enter into their pieces?

Warty tongues caused it. I forced his mouth open, I pulled his tongue out, it was covered with warts, so my friend did magic too. With his warty tongue he covered his round tones with warts, little hard penises. He utters these lizards, everything he points them at comes to life. He thinks too hard at chess, the pieces begin wailing for his milk. He utters fresh tones, covered with nipples. I plead for his secret, he gives me a tongue-kiss. I walk on the beaches, I pronounce a new tide, I wax the moon, I speak a sandcastle, and a child of sand, who turns to me crying, the grains running down his face, his jaw drops and crumbles, his plea rises, from slithering cracks.

28

I am bearded with flowing warts and barbeled with warts. The creatures I make follow in packs for as long as my look stays in their flesh. My way is littered with trees that bleed, and stones that call out from salivating cracks, and ponds that stepped out with assurance and now soak into sand, and a man of bees that looks to me for bibles, and a man of fish and a man of birds like a flying carpet. And Teresa walks in, looks round the room with big hot eyes, and leaves, slamming the door.

VIII

A grandfather clock which is a runic sequence;
A vase full of cool cheese;
A long read of a book in terror and pain;
The grass lawn and its lighted staircases;
A laughing bird with a painted throat;
A fly's cunt modelled in brass and set in a ring;
The art of life drawn in shallow grottoes;
A man's herds, obliterated by stalactite;
Carefully-engraved bear-tracks in the stone floor
Done by the mason in the brain;
The skidding cheer of the fairground audience;
The girl with no scars steps out of her coffin.

The sandy-haired man found life full of interest. In Silas' neckstone he spent much of his time with the radio-set which was connected to the flesh bones penis and brains of the great magician himself. He loved twiddling through the stations and writing down any phrases that struck him particularly. The poem above took him an hour to write with the help of the radio set; it made him feel refreshed, as after a Tarot spread. Now he stepped through one of the doors into Teresa's ring and was relieved to find that she was wearing it. He stood in the sweeping speculum as Teresa cut up her meat and ate. The best times were when she made love to Silas; then the sandy-haired man would stand in the ringstone-

29

window stroking his own penis until they all came together. The next threshold took him to the little hard bloodstone-stroke in the centre of Sarah's head. This was like a bloodstone cottage in a graceful wood of grey willows. Nearby a deep stream ran between clay banks, limpid as air over a clay bed. The air here smelt of earth. He had once slept with one of Sarah's other selves in this cottage, a skinny dark woman with tiny pointed breasts and agile movements, she was writing a book for Sarah, though Sarah didn't know that. The dark girl would step out of Sarah's head when she died and present the book to the judge. She wrote in small bird-scratches on green paper. It was unwise to sleep with other selves. That was exploration downwards through serial bodies. What he was about now was a love-affair with his four people, and they with him. He had thrown the dice on five, and welcomed his fall as he dwindled into the centre spot and fell through the stone. Thus he condensed his life, and if he was to do good, he would shrink these people too. They were so like clouds gesturing high in the air, he wanted stones, rattling against each other, in the bowl of a spring, scouring the bowl, searching into the water, shrinking, the world growing larger and intenser as the foolish complex lives shrank to a point.

two

I saw the red hot mouth of the white bear in the polar cave gaping for me. I struck with my spear: her fingernails on my shoulder looked like a row of red cherries. I lifted her hand gently from my shoulder: I was at a table and there was a row of children in white sitting opposite me and drinking out of gold cups. I raised my silver cup to drink: I was looking out of a deep black egg flecked with gold, I saw through the shell as through a night sky, and I saw the Great Teaspoon glittering down like a scythe. The Great Teaspoon swung down, singing: I was in a street, between a row of mean houses long since condemned. I walked towards them and I saw more clearly that they were not houses but elaborate and ruined well-heads. Far below I saw the glimmer of dark water and a darker circle cut into it by the reflection of my head; a few stars glimmered above. I picked up a stone and dropped it towards that head in the well and I heard a whistling from the sky and I looked over my shoulder at the pitted stone surface rushing towards me. In one of the caves was a man holding up a book for me to see and for an instant I could read the writing which said: I saw the red hot mouth . . . Then he slammed the black covers and all was peace again until the next saint took me up to read, and I was looking up at the stone roof of his cell, and then he took me out in the open air to expound me to multitudes, and then he left me face down on a ledge while he went out to expound me to further multitudes, and I, the book, understood nothing of what he found in me.

And in each hair is a fountain
And beneath each fountain a door
And through each door a river
And in each river a tree
And hanging in each tree a worm
And round each worm a bracelet
And in each bracelet a light
And in each light a horny skull
And in each skull a wand
And in each wand a scroll
And in each scroll a flock of wings
With a squad of dew in each feather
And a lover in each dew
And in the lover a battle
And in the battle hidden fountains
That break within each hair.

What does the fuel think of the flame what does the flame
think of the fire what does the fire think of the ashes sifting
between it it cannot touch (I thought of Tomas) and the
smoke rising out of it it cannot touch or the water that comes
along and quenches it and the earth that is foot-scooped over
its embers. What does the paper think of the ink the ink of
the writer, can the print discern in its own pages the figure of
the saint. I think the print wallows in its own stories. But for
black ink to become bright pictures is morning. And somewhere the saint moves in the ink's landscape, we discern him
in the ink, but he is not made of ink. Sometimes the ink pretends it sees him, sometimes he rushes through touching the
print before the print notices, and only by reading its own
pages a decade later does the print notice footprints still glowing in the mud.

As the lightning struck, the horse's bones glowed brightly
through its skin. Now it takes its fodder from a lighted
brazier. When it whinnies, they are flames, its mouth is a
red-hot grate of bars. In the daytime, in the sunlight, the skin
is dark and leathery and hollow, like a roadman's hutch. In

the dark the fiery glyph which is the true horse standing in its linked bones, shines through.

And I visit my mother Sarah more often now. She is not a saint, so far as I can tell, though she imparts her morning. This spring she has been a small black stone on the beach, and during the great tides she shifted her position often. Sometimes she was a blue stone, and she would wink at me from its invisible centre. All the winter she was a spiral fork-mark in a pat of butter getting dusty on the dining-room table. I invited nobody in that winter, it would have disturbed our relationship. Even before she died, before her bed claimed her permanently, she had for a long time been the inside space of part of the mains water-pipe. This was curiously terrible, since it meant that all the water that came into the house was holy water, even hot bathwater and lavatory water. At first I had a roster or missal of denials that I enjoyed her all over my skin or rinsing my turds carefully before she put them away. I knew these by heart and they insulated me from that enjoyment. Then I gave in and rubbed myself as I squatted on the lavatory and in the hot bath it was my mother! But it was still a relief when she went out on the beach and my sex left the bathroom and went into the sea, and I became a strict scholar and had the house to myself.

I blew the ants into my handkerchief. They started scurrying about like Hebrew scriptures. They ran through the whole corpus of dietary laws in Leviticus in two minutes—I was able to read them as fast as this since I was familiar with them, indeed they made the cavities in my head and for all I knew had bred the ants there. I am the inventor of those lanterns you can buy in Kosher novelty-shops so cunningly built of black wires: by looking through them and twirling them round and round you can read off the whole bible-story in Hebrew. A light burning inside will throw gigantic shadow texts on the wall that change and shift and revise and re-edit themselves. Thus you may read the bible not only as it stands, but the cross-bible too, the middle-bible, the anti-bible and the counter-bible. I had started on an edition of Bach's works for lantern performance when the cavities reminded me I should have to get a new head first. I went to the well in the garden and threw the old pumpkin writhing with maggots under the skullcap into the water. With a gasping a white sopping beard tossed itself over the coping and a high-domed baldness rose into view. I grabbed it and set it on my shoulders. It was the magician's head. I would scry a little.

The crystal ball felt as though it had grown hair suddenly. But the picture was quite clear. In a forest, a seam of clay with a stream running through it and an old man with a white beard digging at the clay with bleeding fingers. Slowly he shaped the figure of a woman. He pulled open his overcoat, his waistcoat, his shirt and plunged hooked fingers into his chest. He withdrew his hand and on the palm waddling and chugging like a frog, his heart was spilling blood in jets. Quick, I thought, put it back or give it to her so she can tend you, but he heard me and slowly turned his face towards the crystal. I looked away quickly but the face still floated in my eyes, hung in the middle of the doorway, rested over the face of the clock on the mantelpiece, swung into the mirror above and with a click settled there as I stood looking at my own face. The beard folded back into the skin which became plumper and rosier and my hair was curly and crisp brown. My face had become so girlish I looked down to see if I still had on men's clothes and I found I was wearing a white shift. I lifted it, I was still male, but clearly much younger. I went out to the garden where the group was waiting for me. There was a sickle moon in the sky as I stood with my cheek to the bark of the pine-tree and my arms squeezing the trunk. He wasn't sure whether the sickle knife had cut a panel in his skull or a slot in his tail. Pain-lightning struck into his darkness. Then the ordinary day came back with a bloody bedsheet, with its little streams and bridges and cups of coffee. He could still remember that instant of last night when the knife opened some slantwise door in him onto a river-land silver like kaolin but streaming with colour, and there was more beneath his feet than above his head, as though most of his sight

34

was in the soles of his feet and in the root of his cock, the great reflections as though he were an ant on a witchball yawing beneath with his striding joints and railway-carriage thorax. The smell of this world was also like a violet colour with the consistency of bone-marrow but bright as sunlight. The pain was still there, like a jagged door that might open at any time. After his breakfast he went out to the pine-tree. He lay down on the pine-needles, a bristling deep couch, looking up at the sky and reaching into the precarious pinnacle of needles. It was fitted together to make a living tree: one of a forest in this space and time. It would fit together needles wherever its seeds sprang, and each needle a pain, and each pain an insight and a joy. Indeed, after his operation the world bristled, and it bristled with pain, and the pain was as rough as stone and as real.

Then he met a girl and wanted to show off. He reached into his purse and took out a white archangel by the hair, which crackled in his grip. Tut he said and put it back quickly, I was looking for what you asked for. His hand throbbed with white pollen. He wiped it clean on a trouserleg. Then he reached into his purse and took out the public hangman; no you don't want him he said and quickly replaced that item. Without ado he reached into his purse and pulled out a large cephalopod; no he said, that isn't right either. He reached into his quaking purse and took out a red madhouse and put it back; it laughed crazily as she shook it; then in rapid succession he brought out a shipwreck, a faithful spouse at the loom, a jar of Loch Ness monster tadpoles, an emblem of virility in the form of the trinity and this was nearly red-hot, four new pence, and a thunderstorm which drowned our voices. Well, don't scoff, my purse is never empty though it may not have what you want, I said, with which remark she twiddled my left breast and I came a world's population out of my purse into her church and the flap at my tail waved like a jagged door in the lightning and she was there too but I was her.

There will come a time when I shall fall into that flapping tail and never come out. Silas-Jonas thought this, so did Teresa and Sarah. The sandy-haired man and Mary and Albert did not. Madness was quite foreign to them. The sandy-haired man was a kind of beetle of the universe, glad to serve as a chess-piece for a few moves, glad to masturbate or copulate, standing quite still as the pain struck, to let it have its way and leave again, acknowledging the joy by leaping into its currents. He knew what it was to be extinguished, caught in crystallising rocks, and to find himself again a million years later, when the iron was smelted. Albert and Mary, Silas' mother and father, had settled for peace. They would pass the problem on, with great benevolence. Their love had settled on Silas' name before he was born. That and the vision of the Hebrew letter on the gate and the raising of strata were the only occasions gates had opened into the world to whose portals Silas was so close. Something about their interior quarrels not taken seriously, even when they flared into rage and occasional petulant violences, something deep as these worlds, had forced Silas into other expedients. It had, for instance, made him very clever at abstract disciplines. At school he was not a schoolboy among schoolboys, able to rage, cry, be betrayed or terrified, take the lead, lose it all in an hour. No, if a single one of those events happened to him he would pick it out and cherish it, take it apart and contemplate it, as an illustration of what he was, a guide into his essential nature. He was good thereby at laboratory science, and loved to be seen with dead books rather than living persons. He became good at this and it won him scholarships. But these mud-thoughts of his developed in parallel, an entry into a world of exciting filth life, a physical world without too many people, yet charged with sexuality. On the one hand, a very clean mechanism; on the other a very dirty little ape. These two had a relationship: mechanism loved the ape with a thoughtful curiosity, a kind of Mr Hyde or Caliban; ape admired

36

mechanism's detachment. A goodish relationship, but an edgy one also, since mechanism felt guilty about ape, and ape mourned the integral virtue that might be his in mechanism, but was not true of either of them. Ape was in many ways the more perceptive. These were the little boy forms of Silas, ape; and Jonas, executive magician. Both were no more than adolescents, though Silas' chronological age was forty.

Jonas had developed a great ritual of washing, which was odd considering Silas' fondness for mud and the like, and of treading in the centre of paving stones to avoid tempting whatever might come out of cracks. Silas had to guess at the contents of books read by himself and Jonas, since Jonas could not turn over a page without praying to god, and, after reading *The White Goddess*, to goddess, to make him a great magician, and not to take his intelligence away from him, to make him a great poet, and before this a great chemist. He couldn't read the books, but he still gained a reputation for learning. This was partly his own desperation and Silas' intuition, but Jonas could never let go. He was afraid of being infected by change, of whatever kind. He was afraid of VD and would wash his hands and rinse his eyes with optrex after going out in the street where he might have met a beggar or a flashily-dressed woman, a breath from whom, a sneeze or even a glance might have given him syphilis of the sensitive love-surfaces of his mouth or eyes. He would put down the date of the encounter in his diary and mark three weeks ahead, by which time the unequivocal signs of the disease would emerge. What he most hated was the silent and invisible spreading of some disease, some change into beggary after having been the richest baby in the world and the most intelligent child, though now there was so much he could not and damn well would not understand. Silas was patient, and had to be, because Jonas was so strong with desperation.

The situation reached its peak in the army service episode. At that time young men were called up to endure eighteen months' national service, and when Jonas found himself in the barrack room, which was like school only much more so, he said to himself 'that's it'. Ignoring Silas, hypnotising him, when the minute violent lance-corporal screamed at them to dismiss one midday Jonas started tottering around the tarmac, saying, where am I? The corporal leaned into his eyes and said, if you're faking! But Jonas was frightened and valiant, he thought that all he needed to do was to get to the doctor. He did so, a major, later an apple-colonel, and he told the major all about his rituals, his incipient ritual magic. Then there was an ambulance, a hospital, many weeks mooning about linoleum corridors, a medical board that insisted he have insulin shock treatment before he was discharged from the army. Discharged from the army! what cleverness. Fu-Manchu Jonas had won.

The shock treatment was sensuous. Lay down on a hospital bed in hospital pyjamas no coverings a mattress with a sheet over it. An injection into the veins of the inside crook of his elbow, which gradually became more and more bruised as the treatment went on. The senior nurse bending over him with the shining needle and his thin clear spectacles. Waking after centuries or no time at all the sheet soaked with sweat and his body aching because he had been in convulsions. He enjoyed all this, and wolfed up the mashed potato they gave each patient after the treatment: insulin snatched all sugar out of the blood and this produced a coma very near to death. The nurses hovered, and when the convulsions ceased and the coma began they gauged the right moment to inject glucose and snatch the patient back from death. Nobody could say why the treatment worked in cases of incipient schizophrenia, which is how Silas-Jonas had been diagnosed, but it did, they said. It didn't for long, apparently, because they later dropped insulin in favour of anti-depressant drugs, and other psychotropics.

Jonas-Silas seemed to thrive, and when they told him this he thought to himself that he loved to please people. The convulsions he was enjoying, the great ejaculation of sweat, became so severe that they changed their procedure slightly, by giving him a draught of luminal before each treatment. The treatments were continuing since he seemed to be enjoy-

38

ing life so much more; naturally, he thought, I have no threat from the army. His rituals continued, and did not abate. Now he could remember some of the dreams. In one he was dead, truly dead, and dissolved into the soil. Later, when he began to write poetry, he didn't see why anything he had done in his life gave him the right to see things that were true in nature. Then he remembered that death had taken him to pieces, that he was conscious of being the mud and soil, that no mythological personages had greeted or punished him.

Lazarus and the sea
The tide of my death came whispering like this
Soiling my body with its tireless voice.
I scented the antique moistures when they sharpened
The air of my room, made the rough wood of my bed, (most
    dear),
Standing out like roots in my tall grave.
They slopped in my mouth and entered my plaited blood
Quietened my jolting breath with a soft argument
Of such measured insistence, untied the great knot of my
    heart.
They spread like whispered conversations
Through all the numbed rippling tissues radiated
Like a tree for twenty years from the still centre
Of my salt ovum. But this calm dissolution
Came after my agreement to the necessity of it;
Where before it was a storm over red fields
Pocked with the rain and the wheat furrowed
With wind, then it was the drifting of smoke
From a fire of the wood, damp with sweat,
Fallen in the storm.

I could say nothing of where I had been,
But I knew the soil in my limbs and the rain-water
In my mouth, knew the ground as a slow sea unstable
Like clouds and tolerating no organisation such as mine
In its throat of my grave. The knotted roots

39

Would have entered my nostrils and held me
By the armpits, woven a blanket for my cold body
Dead in the smell of wet earth, and raised me to the sky
For the sun in the slow dance of the seasons.
Many gods like me would be laid in the ground
Dissolve and be formed again in this pure night
Among the blessing of birds and the sifting water.

But where was the boatman and his gliding punt?
The judgment and the flames? These happenings
Were much spoken of in my childhood and the legends.
And what judgment tore me to life, uprooted me
Back to my old problems and to the family,
Charged me with unfitness for this holy simplicity?

III

Books of reflective and philosophical magic described his
dilemma in exact ways which the psychiatrists did not touch.
But then, he wasn't mad. Jonas was the too much Mercury,
the ritual intellect, the maker of forms. Silas was receiving the
power of Aphrodite and simultaneously the power of the
earth-mother, the mud-mother, and transmitting it to Jonas,
who was afraid of having his mirrors broken. Silas was afraid
of leaving his earth-mother behind, though Aphrodite called to
him with coloured images. Jonas wanted to make maps of
this, Silas wanted to live it. Be not afraid, O nobly-born,
what you see is but yourself, reflected on the mirror of the
void. These were the instructions of the Tibetan Book of the
Dead to the freshly-dead soul. Or there was the Qabalah book
which said that we are now in the sphere of illusion. That
what is about to be described in terms of form are appearances
represented by the intellect to itself and projected back into
the astral light as thought-forms . . . the creations of the
created . . . who will be deceived thereby, if they mistake them
for the abstract essence itself . . . which is not to be found upon
any plane that yields images to psychic vision, but only upon
40

those that are discerned by pure intuition . . . he *represented* to himself the great natural forces . . . whereby they poured into the soul . . . but the force that the image represents . . . is a very real thing indeed.

Then he had better try Jesus. Mary and Albert would like this, and Silas was troubled because he always thought of them as blind people, but there was that clause about pure intuition and no images. He was making these images, was he, in joy and delight as he did, and apparently out of nothing, but in truth out of himself, as a response to the great natural forces in himself and outside. He must not mistake the images for the force, though the images could both transmit and conceal the force, which was only discerned in its essence by intuition. Why, the earth did as much, when the straight sunbeams poured into the grail of waters and the clouds rose and the rain fell leaving the trees and the plants as tracks in their water's course, and the plants leaving their traces which were the fast-moving animals, and the sea full of fish. He could rejoice in the created images and worship what had caused them, it was only his conceit that made him a magician, he would be a poet.

The Force
At Mrs Tyson's farmhouse, the electricity is pumped
Off her beck-borne wooden wheel outside.
Greased, steady, it spins within
A white torrent, that stretches up the rocks.
At night its force bounds down
And shakes the lighted rooms, shakes the light;
The mountain's force comes towering down to us.

High near its summit the brink is hitched
To an overflowing squally tarn.
It trembles with stored storms
That pulse across the rim to us, as light.

On a gusty day like this the force

Lashes its tail, the sky abounds
With wind-stuffed rinds of cloud that sprout
Clear force, throbbing in squalls off the sea
Where the sun stands poring down at itself
And makes the air grow tall in spurts
Whose crests turn over in the night wind, foaming. We spin
Like a loose wheel, and throbbing shakes our light
Into winter, and torrents dangle. Sun
Pulls up the air in fountains, green shoots, forests
Flinching up at it in spray of branches,
Sends down clear water and the loosened torrent
Down into Mrs Tyson's farmhouse backyard,
That pumps white beams off its crest,
In a stiff breeze lashes its tail down the rocks.

IV

Then he had better try Jesus. His college had taught him to
evoke the Saviour as a protection, as a matter of form, and
one of the great paths on the tree of life was said to evoke him
or his avatars, and it was part of the magician's training to
work these paths by imaginative and sensuous realisation,
with the aid of symbols and rites, just as a Jungian psychiatrist will apply what he calls active imagination to a patient's
dream. In the latter instance the symbols of the dream would
be used: the patient might dream of a locked door, and the
doctor would say, imagine the feel of the threshold under your
feet and of the key in your hand, put the key in the lock and
open the door. Now say what you see. Or write it. The
magician would use symbols that were reputed to be of im-
memorial antiquity, of the Qabalistic tree of life, a glyph of
the tree from which Adam plucked the fruit, according to the
rabbis, and those of the Tarot cards. This would give the
magician control over the deepest levels of his own mind. But
Silas, like Faust, didn't want control any more. That was
Jonas. Silas wanted knowledge of what he was in himself.
And he had better take Jonas with him, since he was a part of

it. Silas wanted knowledge, but the knowledge of the creature for the creator, if that were possible. He did not want to put himself first. So he must use no implements, no formal invocations or robes. The paths in the College from Mercury, that was Jonas, to the Sun, that was Jesus, lay by the way of knowledge of the Devil; from Aphrodite and the coloured sexual travels of Silas to the Sun was by way of the knowledge of Death; and the way from Jonas to Silas was by way of the falling tower.

The falling tower
Up all these stairs, upon all these landings,
On the topmost floor he broods, all eyes,
Lensed in windows of plain clear glass,
Re-lidded with striped curtains, broods
Upon the outside, the inwards full of books
Brooding on themselves till opened. Outside
Is squandering and charging and recharging, oh,
Tulips, boils, soiled capes, chimneys,
Stern people in damp socks, privet, poses,
A world of types. But then – to rejoice
In the sudden cowering of a cowl of smoke, a sparrow
Exploding like a puff of blades up lives of rain,
Alighting solid, tapping down the tiles that pulse –
Or in wide windows uttering heads that tug and lean
Towards the hoarse and jangling rag-bone man who
Fondles his mouth with loudness, and to be thrust up
On foundation-piles of years, repeated
Packing-cases, beer-mugs, shawls, expounding – to be riding
  high
On heaps of babyhood and suddenness
Presiding with one's eyes alight . . . and then
To be engulfed, inverted, slipped inside-out
And fall beneath the focus of a mountain
Of books and boots and chamber-pots, newsprint, seedcake,
Of all that's passed before, within one, to lie
In galleries of excremental furniture – that swoops again,

Back-to-front degulfs, enthrusts, peaks up
The unthinking furniture of a tall young house
With one's far-seeing, afloat, enthroned,
Squatting in the sky's abyss,
Its focus, where clouds are personal and kindly
Secreting their moist happiness, and to breathe
Among attentive books plumb in the eye of it, looking out
To where the other half-million
Sit in the apple of their sky's eye . . .
And then to rejoice.

He hoped his experiences under insulin shock had helped him
with the dying. He was desperately afraid of the devil. The
poem of the falling tower said nothing about his suspicions
that Silas was him being an unconfident woman, and Jonas
was animus, a not-very-good-man: it only remarked the depressions and the Tarot image, which he had not at first
thought of as a bisexual image, until Teresa had dreamed it as
the chimney of her womb. He hoped that when he brought his
shrinking person under the glare of these forces he could read
by an evoked intuition what they so rapidly were saying. But
why was he so hesitant? Admittedly he had never invited
Jesus or the image of him to cavort in his mind before. It was
because Sarah and Teresa were very much involved. He
wasn't trying to spook and be spooked any more. If that was
all they wanted, what would happen? Or perhaps he was giving up all power to them, and he would be nothing but a bowl
of reflections, spooked up completely. He had to die in these
lands, to find the country where you woke up. And he was
making too much fuss.

v

Yes, I saw Jesus and he took the bible down from the lectern
with an easy shrug of his heavily-muscled shoulders and in
one hand and I thought he was going to tear the great book
in half but instead he unfolded it into a tree. His hand caught

44

in the partly-unfolded pages and they ran up his arm like fire or tendrils and I said, Look out Jesus! and he threw his other arm up in a gesture of alarm and as he threw it up to the sky it budded with leaves and his feet rooted and his head folded back into the trunk and as it went back it just managed to say, Abba, and disappeared in a spray of spit. Then there was silence and I was standing in front of this special tree on a forest path and the sun sprinkled through the leaves. There was a rustling above my head. I thought it was birds but it was a serpent and I could not understand its high voice like a woman speaking to me, so I turned away. But then a bass voice started singing to me saying that he wanted me to become the forest and its roots and fruits but that sounded to me too much like a family tree. Even so I turned back to the tree and I saw a grand city opening its gates to me.

But such a waft of bad air came out at me through these gates I said be damned to this. Then my sight cleared and I saw the serpent with its jaws opening. There were sharp teeth and lightning inside. I drew back suddenly silvery with sweat and running with shivers as the smell changed in a peculiar way that I liked, like armpits in the ceremony, so I said, Jesus himself wouldn't have opened the book for me if he hadn't meant something to happen so I stepped inside. Inside there I learnt how not to breathe. After I learnt that I was shown an apple on a tree, the apple was pulsing and the tree was a ladder of bone and I realised that I had the serpent's heart in my hand so I bit into it. The juice was a bloody froth and I was jerked off my feet by the convulsions and then the cold grew around me and the clammy folds settled and I was on a hospital bed on a soaking sheet and Jimmy was still having convulsions in the next bed and my back hurt. I looked down at myself and I wanted to tear into my body with my hands to find the thing that made worlds and then I felt like breadcrumbs and I could see all the messages streaming down the nerves from the eyes in the skin and the raw places.

A 60 mph rhinoceros stampede – thousands of rainbow-coloured mice – hair – fog – all the sounds of the sea – Jonah and the Whale and the Sea – Mount Everest – and the sands of the desert – blasts of freezing air that spangle my hair and moustaches – hurrying eyes, scarves and teeth – butter melting – all the world's great reptile-houses – saliva – beetle-juice – aspirins and mummy's voice saying that a bullet was the fastest cure for a headache – Niddip, niddip, niddip and the oozing spectre of the fat frog-prince – glistening marrow along bone – the debris of a train-crash, glass in bucketfuls, crumpled girders, tea-urns and door-panels, British Railways uniform stuffed with human hamburger – candlegrease moving in great tiers, balconies, stairways and dripping valances – an infinite tiger's tail studded with rubies – tombstones muttering epitaphs – money – facepowder – druids – flights of birds and flights of arrows and flights of birds and flights of arrows – cones of silence – rainbows – time – an endless polished sabre-blade slashing at heads – an endless red tongue, rough and stained – the bible-story told in a continuous stream of stained-glass windows – showers of steel knitting-needles – moths and grapesize vole embryos – asses' milk and dead men's fingers – a continuous display of men's hand-painted silk neckties – a white spout pulsing with downward-pointing bands of scarlet – a fat stream of heavy shining mercury – honey, thick with bees' corpses and fragments of wax, a massacre in sunshine – a spout of shining pearl-colour, which branches as it runs and makes its own pathways – Aussies with bayonets shouting, we mike our own 'oles – buttons rattling through, ivory, bone, painted porcelain, leather diamanté, toggles, reflecting mirrors, emeralds, sapphires, topaz, chrysoprase, moonstone, chalcedony, turquoise, peridot, tourmaline – expectation ripped by sniggers ripped by chuckles ripped by guffaws and then riotous white applause-noise dying to expectation – mother-jelly with the eggs of scorpions – streaming thunderclouds – soft human ashes running as through an hour-glass – stars – black molten lava full of white screaming maggots – acorns and freezing air and dead leaves and peals of bells and little withered apples –

46

In the house of the Reverend Earth and Dr Waters
Moonlight strikes from the taps!
In the daytime, it is sunlight, full clear beams of it!
When they give water, these faucets, it is holy water,
Or river water, with green shadows of great ship-hulls glid-
ing in it.
There are some also that bundle out exceptional ripe golden
cornsheaves
And blackberries also, and pineapples and nightshade and in-
numerable other kinds of berries.
There is a large curved one like morning glory full of strong
birdsong
And the smell of woodsmoke mixed with wet nettles.
Others I would not turn on again, not if you paid me, there
are some
That throw out glittering lead, or rushes of fire,
And these are all made of wood, so that they smoke and
scorch as they run,
And if they char too far they can never be turned off again.
There is another which is the faucet of pouring darkness,
my eyes dim,
I grope, can I ever find it again to stop the darkness coming?
And there is yet another and this is the worst that seems to
give out nothing
But when you look round there are certain articles missing.
But mostly they give out good things, sunshine and earth,
Or milk, or fine silky stuffs that glide out rustling,
The sleepy evening sounds of a town on the edge of the
country
With rooks cawing as they settle, the clank of a pail, a
snatch of radio music,
(Though I remember another that turned on a soft a con-
tinuous cursing
And from it extruded a pallid foul-mouthed person
Whose mouth foamed as I turned him off at the chest . . .)
But so many of them turn out good things, there is no
majority

Of flowing blood or raw gobbets of flesh, it is mostly
Womansong, a stream of laughter or of salmon or bright blue
  pebbles –
And the lion-headed spigot that gushes mead and mead-hall
  laughter –
There are so many giving moonlight and in the day bright
  sunlight, rich dark barley-wine, and dew . . .
In this house of personages that prefer tenants to use the taps
  and sample the waters
And best of all to install faucets running with their own
  personal tastes and choices,
In the great house of the Reverend Mrs Earth and Doctor
  Waters

VI

Teresa mumbled to herself out walking, I did not want to
read Silas' poems to the old lady. My voice went winding in
to the wooden flower of Sarah's ear. I cannot understand
his poems when I read them to anybody else, I must read
them to myself. I felt like a man reading. I want them for
myself. I should not have slivered myself to Sarah, like steal-
ings in the water; the crests of waves like crowds snatching
white books open to read. I was coming to myself halfway
through a poem and losing myself again. The wooden
flower points at me, it wags, it chirrups, I have been asleep
and mumbling. Then the book blooms again under my
gaze. Somewhere the sense is falling, not in my head, in that
half-opened drawer of cotton-reels, among the sheet music,
caught on the cactus, I don't like to think of all the coloured
Aphrodite's pictures it is making in Sarah's head. The old
watermill is working again as she passes by it: Silas would
make a Frankenstein poem out of the old man who lives
there, she thinks.

From: Doktor Baron Victor von Frankenstein,
The Frankenstein Clinic,

48

Karlstadt,
Nr. Munich, Germany   February 20th, 1870

My Dear Niece,
I am writing to you from our clinic's new library. I am
sitting among my patients, just like one of them. Professor
Poe's withdrawal symptoms are gathering above his head
again like brightly-coloured tree-foliage and bunches of oyster-
shells tied together with slowly-moving pictures. I have pre-
scribed a nubian vizier to stand behind him at all times. He
lops the growth off with his scimitar when it becomes too
cumbersome.

Our library's toad is heavy. It gazes at the linoleum. It
carries a small castle of spectacles on its back. I have seen
toads gone grey with the carrying of this castle. In the last
sunlight they creep like ghosts of smoky amethyst. I am a
reader here often. The chapters are rapidly-moving beams of
light. The letters of the alphabet are like little vials swiftly
filling up with a slow clear poison. I have seen toads carrying
grey flasks of smoke. In this library the dirt-secrets lie in
layers, like oyster-beds. I open such a book; its cool sinlight
pours up, and the sea-bed is alight. The toad completes its
rounds, pauses to pant, and starts off round the room once
more. I believe the chapters multiply afresh each night. I believe that to open a book pulls a string in the librarian's head
that starts him cataloguing new books. The toad pauses at the
edge of my table and to oblige him I take new lenses and slip
them into my spectacle-frames. This enables me to flinch at
the clear lightning of the dirt-jokes. I grow tanned and swarthy
indeed in this electrical sunshine. I shall soon be fit for the
outer world again, and enabled to understand the dirt-jokes.
Though my hands are worn away and as thin as the pages
they turn all day. The toad keels over like a beanbag, its
casket of lenses splashes crystal on the floor. It is quite dead.
He was a schoolmaster. His name was Buffon. Half-a-dozen
blueflies that were doing duty for initial letters rise from my
page at the clatter, circle buzzing, and settle again, in fresh

49

positions. The page now has another meaning which I read to myself with zest, since the more dirt-secrets I know and the funnier they are the better I shall be qualified to move about in the world. Air hisses from the corpse of the toad, but the flies do not take fright, and his leathery corpse collapses in quiet folds. He will be allowed to dry, when his belly will fall open on his spine in many slices which are the natural pages, and then any person will be able to read the meaning of his life, and where it is not clear the blueflies and smaller insects will fill out with a laughable and smutty meaning, the librarian will gilt-tool him with some arbitrary title, and the one invariable legend, Beelzebub's library at the Frankenstein Clinic.

So you see, my dear dirt-girl, what pains we are at to keep ourselves busy at the Clinic. Are you wearing a soiled dress today? Please write and describe the stains you put on at breakfast.

Your affectionate uncle
Victor von F.

From the prospectus of the von Frankenstein Clinic:

. . . . . To say the least I was impressed by my visit. He must be a most learned man. I visited one of his research departments, which is a cross between a greenhouse, a library, a laboratory, a machine tool shop and a chamber of horrors. I noticed a glittering shape in one of his alcoves, like a pile of silver money, or a Christmas tree. It was a human skeleton modelled out of tinsel. No! said Frankenstein, his hand detaining me, his keen eyes glittering over his precise lips and clean-cut jaw. Do not touch that, Herr Professor. Not yet. That is a model of all the man-making star-convergences that obtained at my birth. It is alive in its own right. Look at this portrait – pointing to one miniature in a long row – it is the baby of the man you see before you (settling his chin more comfortably in his high stock). We are conceived at the

50

moment that certain stars shine, and intersecting in this moment's form, they imply us totally. I am the unwinding of this complex comb, one instant of which you see before you, others of which are glimpsed in the miniatures and daguerreotypes on this wall. The tree is made within a light-sensitive solution of tin contained in a special camera, my father set the camera to take a picture of the night sky from his bedroom window in the moment that I was conceived. At the instant when he felt my mother coming, he allowed himself to come, and switched the cape from the camera. As each star ray travelled through the fluid, its action deposited a thin rod of tin. Each year my father had a fresh portrait made, and a fresh picture taken. When I die, my son will take pictures, and he will watch the stars that made me no longer converging, but pulling apart from each other to go their separate ways creating new people . . .

VII

As the silver combs drew apart, the sandy-haired man walked quickly from Teresa's ring into Silas' neckstone. He stood in the great window looking down Silas' body. The cock was limp in its forest, the nipples on either side of him gradually lost their pink colour as much of the blood drained from them, then grew darker as the capillary blood began to grow stagnant. They were of course motionless. Through the flooring of the pendant he could feel the crackle like basketwork easing when a load is taken out of it: the crepitation of the cell-walls as their constituents changed, as the heat went out of them, as the nimble liquid fat became solid lard, as their own enzymes began to eat holes in them. Even in the white light of the sheet that covered the body he could see that the skin was growing whiter, and the black hair blacker. The sandy-haired man lifted his own neckstone and looked into it. There he could see the sheeted figure laid out on the hospital table. With an impatient gesture he put the stone in his mouth and bit it off; then he turned and walked quickly through the

51

door into Teresa's ring. Once there, he wound a facet-window down a little, leant his head out and spat the stone warmed in his mouth into the bowl of the spoon Teresa was lifting to her gigantic lips. He watched and heard her suck it down, wound up the window. Then he kissed his finger to her, walked to a black door at the back of the ring, it closed and he was gone.

Tomas had persuaded Teresa to drink a little of her soup. What will you call the child? he asked. She didn't reply. She was thinking what sex magic could possibly be, and how Mary was immaculately conceived, and how Mary then had Jesus by Virgin birth, without a man. So that meant that St Anne had made the first station, by bearing Mary without birth-trauma, since birth-trauma is the Fall, the forgetting by fear and terror of the existence in the womb. This meant that Mary remembered how she herself grew, and she therefore could grow one of her own cells into Jesus, and more than that, be with him in the womb. Silas taught me by path-working to remember my birth, and to endure my birth. I will now grow my Silas for myself and be with him as he grows.

There are no words for this. Only change. One thing moving to another, a feeling moving into a sensation, and the rate of its shape of change, and moving back into a thought which becomes an intuition. The stars' tree is always changing, and the scale, and when we wake it is a simplifying dream, a kind of death in which we invent a language. We are surprised to find great and far-reaching kindnesses reflected deep within this language. Poetry is the calculus of growth, and intuition is how we articulated ourselves, through all those dangers, and the final shock-gate of growth, the birth, where most of us forgot ourselves, for ever. No one can deceive themselves, or be mad themselves, or become insane. They can be out of contact with it, shocked into life which is too much for the grey shocked core called brain.

We resent the negro race, because they move with spaces between their bones. We resent this, it seems both secretive and showy. We resent it because it is sexual, it is free easy fucks, it

52

is free easy shits, it is free easy births without penalty. It is bodily intuition, it is the intuition with which the body grew itself. That is on the level of physical body; on the levels of feeling and imagination it is rite and custom and magic. There the dead are very close, in the bush of ghosts, and the bush of ghosts is in the belly of the pregnant woman. The newly-dead and the not-yet-born are very close, and the ancestral dead and the gods are alive in the cells of each person, and the rites feed them, so they know who they are. Whitey will not have the sun, the grey-pink brain is seen in the skin, and the skin is the same substance as the brain: in the embryo it is ectoderm. Ectoderm is infolded to become brain in the foetus. Black feeds on the brain when it is an inner sun, and on the sun outside, with a black skin, which is a container of great depth. Silas-Jones, who died so in insulin shock, was the last white man. He died in the attempt to recover what was lost to the white races and described in their doctrines of the Fall, which the coloured races do not share. The Fall was to pluck the grey brain-fruit instead of the sun-bloody heart-fruit. It is the labyrinth of inhibition which robs their children of the natural memories of what they were. God rages in their bibles because they have got so far from him with their decisions and personalities. Jesus on his cross showed where God was and how to obey him. To this day the figure on the crucifix leans his head to the right, as the baby is born the head rotates to the right just so. Jesus is retracing his path, and the cross is the open legs and the spread genitals of his mother. The white races carried this utterance and instruction of their hero about with them for two thousand years without getting the message: it was the only way he could put it into one word which would not be lost. It was not lost, it was preserved, exactly as uttered, and that was all, until the best men of the white races grew split and grotesque and withered with self-abasement or exploded with inflation, like stones or like gesturing clouds, not like men born of women born of the earth born of the sun born of space. Teresa is black and joins her sun-child in the womb, and they converse with

53

feelings and small rapidly-created universes. Not sex only, not magic only, not poetry only, not madness at all, but womb-talk, the first conversation of the growing spirit with the life that lives it and the death it will die into life with its bride the earth.

Teresa learnt Silas-Jonas' magic. He did not understand it himself, he did not know what it was. She had no need to learn it; he recalled it in her. Now she carries not his, but her own child. It will be herself. But it will also be her child of the idea of Silas.

three

My hand is wrapped in a bloody cloth. I carry the small clock which bleeds like the head of a baby through the corridor levels. They wind like a shell. The shell echoes with the throbs of great clockwork. I step out into clockwork. It is like scaffolding and the shadows of scaffolding emitting scaffolding. It is like axes falling and heads tumbling and knots tightening.

I am here to offer the small clock to the great one. I put the small clock on the tooth of a cog the size of a church rose-window that revolves in mesh with a pudgy companion the size of a cow's head. Tooth greets tooth and my small clock is metal feathers and a screech and a pattering.

The screech is like a baby's wail at baptism. I am a clock-maker, and a midwife to the mineral kingdom. I build the small clocks inside the great one in my workshop the shape of a shell pointing downwards, and my circular watch-bench is in the lowest coil at the tip, I make travelling clocks in the next tier, alarm clocks in the next level, mantelpiece clocks in the next, and grandfather clocks in the greatest space.

When I have built the small clocks I carry them out into the village of the great clock. I sacrifice them in the great clock's munching entrails. Each time I do this the clock is stripped of its materiality and in the suddenness of its absence, in this absence which is full of the skill of my building, god rushes. A child is conceived, somewhere. A child that was once a pile of rocks in my smelting works, copper, iron, tin, and then a clock that twitched and counted and chimed.

My chief enemy is the great clock. I hate him. His monstrous ego. His executioner's attitude. The throb which is a clang. His refusal to become flesh and blood.

I wait for the hurt. The blow he strikes every hour. I drop the bloodstained cloth (how eager that little clock was to become human! its tick that was so shrill to begin with slowly dropped in pitch until it was a moan, then dark clotted blood). I straighten my tie. I stand straighter. He strikes with a terrible roar like lions from a bell the size of the British Museum, a hideous explosion which must loosen as it rattles through the many storeys of mincing movement, which almost shudders me off my girder (a little blood oozes from my ear), which echoes downwards through spokes and galleries, the hairspring the size of a greyhound track which responds with its own chorus of jangling chords. Surely the monster will shake itself to pieces one day with its own voice! the thoroughfare of metals die! What a human it would make, so purged of mechanism, timeless after counting so much time here, so serene a human from this mechanism if it would bend its mountainous head and take death at its own hand.

So much of her theology sounds like gossip. Perched up on the lectern, festooned in her qualifications, preaching, she distils lechery into the gospel stories. And yet she denies it. Clean jaw-line, an expression of intelligent surprise, a thin and withered air, and a mezzo-soprano public manner. They flock to her. All the men think of themselves: each a Jesus-man in smouldering robes, a crooner with extra-terrestial divinity; all the women unrepentant Magdalens, goddesses with super-numerary nipples, their god found and their cunts gaping. Everyone, myself included, ruminating on the gossip that will be written about me. Bound into soft leather covers for people to take the sortes from. My accidental doings oracles for everyone's advice. She is the reason why women preachers were not allowed. And she takes it too far. She says she doesn't intend it, doesn't want it, she tells the stories plain and interprets according to how the Holy Spirit moves her. But the first crooning caress of the mezzo, like thick blue

56

brush-strokes on a naughty nursery door, wets the cunts and hoists the pricks of the holy audience.

As he listened to her he thought: Jesus' life was so charged. My life could be charged like this. I say impatiently to the old phoney 'Take up your bed and walk'. He gets up and hobbles off because he's afraid. I roll my eyes like crucibles in a furnace, my words lope over the dust to him like Chinese writing in flames. My words create pictures in him, nobody else did that. Lazarus was dying of inanition. He was a catatonic, a hebephrenic, a schizophrenic. The devils had dug him out. His cock had grown up and the mother in him wanted it too much. He couldn't allow that and clenched himself to death. Jesus unclenched him by telling a dirty story of a tender kind. Then laid his hands gently on his cock and brought him off. Jesus desired Magdalen, the woman taken in adultery. But he said so, he described to the other watchers, each with a stone in his hand, how beautiful she was, and they saw it, and their clenched hands grew limp from beauty, and the stones fell to the floor.

And she makes us so angry that our heritage is no more than this bible, and even this ought to be printed with a warning, as on the cigarette-packets, that it may be dangerous to health; or a warning that 'You do not understand the meaning of most of what happens to you. You can barely remember the greatest things. A great thing happened to us; we were in love with this man. You think we should tell you this plain? Then try to describe your own great dreams or your best sex. You will find that they are all so self-evident as you do them, so impossible to remember completely, so rebellious to description. We do not understand the meaning of these pages. They are notes taken as we were waking from a good life into this life, something we hoped to bring with us.'

The bonfires, building marble columns beneath the trees. The flow of the snail-shell, the endless unwinding torrents of it. The boulder, one knot in the storm. He took the teeth of the giants and carved scrimshaw bolsters of them, and scrimshaw urns. He thought so fast about water that it went slow and he would walk on its ridges like a ploughed field. The sun was drilling caves in the icy sea and in the glacier. Moses' horns span and drilled commandments into his forehead; he could not rest with the pains and led his people. His beard was flame and his face was fuel. He touched the window and it burst like a soap-bubble. The iron bird muted shot-droppings, it winged its slow way through the rock-strata. He trod the three-ton carpet of the sperm-whale's tongue. He spoke so slowly it was the cocking of a rifle in silent woods, the chiming of the grandfather clock in the closed house: his lips writhed round his filed teeth like saplings growing through a long summer.

But he shoots the dog like slamming a door on it.
Should I therefore cherish the thing that is growing?
The fern unrolls as the bishop's staff does not.
His mitre pretends to a cloven head and red fertile soil inside.

The congregation of children smells of freshly-baked bread. There were doors constructed of revolving blades to shear the grass. Death has a scythe, it is the mirror-step of a door-way. I see myself coming towards me. Now I have no shadow, I am dead. He shoots himself like slamming a door. Lions fear the creaking of carriage-wheels; love fears the farce, the slamming of doors. So many minerals weaving this solid room, rigid scarves, and no door visible.
    The jaws of paradise?
    No. Brightly-coloured butterflies over a quagmire. A pocket of sweet smells. A pocket of foul smells. That was the first. The second apparition was a notice in the chemist's window. Steedman's Praying Powders. The next, near the abandoned mines at St Day, was The Tor Glass. A gigantic boulder-sand glass more than a mile high thundering and lightning. Who would turn it around when it had had its say? The bad weather passed away at length. The disused shafts still re-sembled empty sleeves. The sleeper would one day don them.

And he hated his head when it thought and saw like this. I just have an awkward kind of head, he declared, slapping its temples, slapping its temple hard. I get nothing from the books I read, the cinema, from history, facts slip through, I just get vertigoes and apparitions, apparitions and vertigoes. Things are easing, he said. Only the police and the universities really mind nowadays.

Members of the Vesuvius Ensemble join today with the Burning Philharmonic Orchestra and the Asmodeus Quartet . . . the giant magistrate nods his head with a ringing of gongs . . . the log-tables, he found after his long reveries, had melted in his fingers to scented oil and angelica . . ., the two conductors disagreed as to whether it should warble or pierce at that point . . . the radio-set is a small electrical press, the music it exudes is an intoxicant prepared from crushed fresh-air . . . ripe stars in dew-streaming chariots . . . one solitary cloud glides out of a mountain-cave . . . tiny sighs infest the darkness like seeds . . . mud tramps in, cheering us all with his green festive quips . . . a wasp-nest shaped like a heart and kept on a gold chain and given a hutch and fed on cider and strawberries . . . no, my dear, I was not dozing, I heard every word you said perfectly.

He paused at the print of the woman's buttocks where she had slipped in the mud. A gigantic kiss. He caught up with her at the shaman's clearing. A seamonster was disappearing into the headdress known as 'The Mystery of the Sea'. The shaman was wrestling with a spirit that resembled a continually-falling cliff. He danced to keep his footing as he struggled over the pouring talus. The man was full of mud-feelings, slippery and capacious. He whispered into the woman's ear 'Come back with me to the mud'. She smiled and began to speak angrily, but the shaman approached. He touched her on the shoulder and pointed towards his hut. She lowered her eyes and went submissively, followed by the skinny naked magician, who took no notice of the young man, who frowned, made as if to follow her, then thought better of it and left the clearing. He went back to the mud-patch, and knelt by the doubleprint. There was no mistaking they were hers, he thought, as they slowly filled with water and disappeared.

The typewriter is suddenly too big. I try moving the table. A muddy green-shirted pond appears where I want to put the chair. There are ducks on it. The typewriter has grown as large as a barn and emits cattle-lowing. Hens are roosting on some of the keys, straw starts out between them. The door in the typewriter opens and out slouches a terrible-looking cow with great slack udders, strings of saliva swinging from her mouth and plastered buttocks, and a brindled barking across her back which reads 5/8. : and I follow heavily. K wanders past, her tail swinging; E lurches into the hedge. I realise that if they go back to the field, if they escape, I have lost the works of my typewriter. I raise my arms and run towards them shouting, they wheel and scamper weightily, then round the corner of the barn comes a woman in khaki jodhpurs shaking a stick at me: they must rest and feed, she shouts.

A small skiff hailed us. It was full of uniformed children. 'Can we board you?' We had no alternative. Land was out of sight in the usual mist. When they were safely on board I slipped into the sea and paddled round to where their boat was hung on davits. I reached up and folded it in my arms. I bent it in half and the hull stove in. Then I pulled myself up on the deck and went in search of the children. One by one I squeezed their hard little throats until they died. My emotion was mild. I squeezed, I closed my eyes, I was a woman, the broomstick between my legs, I held it in front of me with my throttling grip. Then I opened my eyes. The white linen cap had fallen on to the deck from the head of the little corpse. I thought that the door to the invisible, the door that guarded it, must be just as visible as that fallen cap.

Now I put more of myself together. The hat goes on my head. I pick the grey rag out of the bucket, wring it out, it will do for a brain. The rest of me is like ragged seaweed through which my white legs come, and my arms. Force-meat savours are streaming through me from the ripped tissues. I ask for the original script. I am in a raw state and it is difficult to read. I pick up the sentences like fillets of black fish. I turn them over and I swallow them. They give up their meaning. You can see through the pages. This is the moment in the day which Satan can't find. I come out of its doorway and instead of pain it is all images again. I have a weakness, it is an allantois. There is derision which does not speak, the rim of the beaker is cold. There is a trench we have a pick I want the feline serpent just there tie that lace here is a nookhome a quaver quince and sugar secret devices all is going a weal over a well I dig shelves with obsolete boots it is almost free I shall forget that.

The green thing with the gold crown lives in the pond. The virgin idiot laid in the mud at the edge which was his love. Now the green thing with the gold crown lives there. Gather me bones, verger. The lady thing came all voluptuous and slippery out of the green pond and there was a gold crown among the waterweed. She rose from beyond the margin of rushes but her legs buckled and she fell on her smooth un-featured face. Give her legs, said the vicar and the verger held out a bundle of bones and the slime snatched them and stood on them. Now the snub-nosed skull and the lady had a face with green eyes. Vicar stepped forward with green shirt and skirt but the lady brushed him aside and went on towards the west under the green trees in the last sunshine. The pond gaped black water-cave behind her.

The snail, its stonejersey shell gave it the look of screaming. No, the snail crept into the sun-love, it crept out under the blue and the gull, into the criss-cross, the checkerwork, the love played raw chess onto it, so its skin heaped a tall fort-ress upon it. The love-light pincered the tip of the snail's back, it spun petrification downward. Jennic gasped. In the love-light the snail spoke. It spoke a small violet flower. It spoke a short thrush – a chat, a phrase. It spoke a small violet flame

61

that crossed to the bush. Then it drew itself to its full height and spoke an angel, who decayed, like oil spreading holes of rainbow over an upright river. It spoke, 'celestial chicken', and a frog survived the decomposition of the river and sat quaking. Then it said, 'a tall beast-tower', and a crate of eggs was laid on the doorstep. It said, 'a ladder of green trees', and the convolvulus wound upwards out of sight round the dust-bins. It said, 'wealth', and all consolation disappeared in a sound like milk-bottles and the world's work began again. These were the bad answers the devil gave.

This morning, Lammas-tide, I had my annual postcard from the Society for Blue Mud. The photo on the front was one of the great scrimshaw ceremonial chalices brimming with hot blue clay. I remember the hall of the mistai, the rows of clay-packed coffins, stalked with one straw for breathing, the dishes of mercury at chest-height which the Practicus in charge would inspect through his clean thin spectacles for the tremblings that announced the rebirth pangs. Then the successive crashes as they fell off their trestles and the clay smashed, the postulant struggling free from the dusty lumps, to be helped up and given a dish of food, and escorted to the baths.

In those struggles, every candidate dreamed, and his special friend, his initiator and he would go over and over the dream, to interpret it. The result might be nothing, it might be a new name for the candidate, it might be a new meaning to his life.

I had been through the ordeal more than a few times. Unfortunately I had got a feel of the sticky clay on me, and I couldn't get it done to me enough. The elders could not decide whether this gave me a special merit, or whether I was just stuck at the threshold.

Some never emerged. Their wedges of clay containing their bodies were fired in the kiln, and placed aside in the pile of building-bricks. Those who emerged kept a memento of their struggle, the impression of imperturbable lips in blue glaze, or that of a sleeping eye. Heretical, I practised copromacy, turning my dung blue with methylene blue capsules, with the comfortable feeling that even if I was not at the moment passing through my favourite trials, they were passing through me.

The dog ran along the beach with a shock of seaweed in its mouth. I remembered Stanislaus, who was a skeletoniser. Obsessive. We would go for a walk together, and he would skeletonise the leafy trees, imagining every scrap of green flesh gone. A wood of cobwebs and staves. The axons and transistors of a great grey computer. The look of the sunlight piercing so many tiny holes would grow wolf-fur on our skins and we'd start to run. Then he'd point to a woman getting off a bus. Do you see the ankylosed shoulder-joint? It can't roll properly, she walks in her way because of it, she sidles up to people in her way because of it, it moves in an angular way, not in a woman's way, and she will choose only certain sexual postures because of it. It is visible only to the minute observers of skeletons, and yet on it grows her stance to life. By this time I could see the identical pleasant grin that spread itself below the flesh of all the shoppers, with their sharp elbows.

He had invented a fluid that would draw aside the flesh like muddy curtains from the bones of any animal. A thick and fluid cream, that crackled and rumbled when he tipped the dead kitten into it. He was a watchsmith of bones, preferring delicate articulation, the feathery animals, though he had tackled lions for the zoo. As he made love to me I felt melted so only my helpless bones were left. When I jilted him he said, that fontanelle in your forehead. It's beginning to close at last.

I read articles in the papers about him before long. He had discovered another fluid that would dissolve rocks, but not their inclusions; that, laid like thick paste on a stretch of rock, would develop as in a photograph, and expose the fossil bones of dinosaurs and the delicate plates of crinoids. Then the diamond people used it on their blue clay, and it would dissolve a clay face, leaving nothing but a shingle of gems.

63

He disappeared shortly after I read this. He left his skeletons to the nation. Walk into the Natural History Museum and you will find in the entrance, in the Great Hall, a very white tall skeleton on a plinth pointing with ultimate arm towards the hall of insects, those beings who always wear their skeletons on the outside, and surrounded, more naked than Adam, by flocks of skeletonised animals in natural postures.

His is the only human scaffolding in the collection. I believe it is his, and that he found the secret of life after death, and that one dark night he, being out of the flesh, put himself together with his usual skill. I inspected the exhibit minutely, with a powerful lens, and on the occiput I found engraved a message for my eyes alone: 'Grown up at last. Here's looking at you, love. S.'

On rising to his feet again he was no longer the saint. He looked down at himself, the realisation of what had happened fading with that which knew it in him. He was a man for whom the morning jug or pail was a friend, the collie in the corner shop; the convicted murderer who visited him under guard, for psychoanalysis, was especially a friend. He lived in the world of the saints, but, truly, he thought himself mad. What is this, he said to himself, when every little thing, a grain of dust in a shell, or a seaside tavern, looks at me with a countenance, with a face of such friendly openness I have to cry out 'Goodday, Friend!'; or with a look of such suffering that I must either run past it or kneel and embrace it. And people! Every wrinkle, every quiver, is a sentence that changes and writes another meaning and goes on declaring itself. And I stand up to those quivering volumes of meaning and I say 'I'm mad, I think. Please, can you help me?' Sometimes they can. Often they can't hear what I mean.

Everybody he met would be faced with the question. 'Have you the cure? Have *you* the cure?' And the people around gave their madness to him to cure himself with, expounded their mad theories about the meaning of life or the impossible

64

ways they had been tricked and cheated, and all the madness flowed into him and through him, and he inspecting it for that least particle of true madness that could cure him of his. And one morning, sitting on the edge of his bed, in the bare room with the unpatterned wallpaper with which he used to converse since it looked so miserable, in the room where he listened to the murderer psychoanalysing him, and this healed the murderer, looking back over the day – he found that tiny grain of true nonsense, and he took it up and his mind inspected it and it ran through his mental fingers like the hot blood and like tendrils and flowered in his prick and flowered upwards into his brain and bushed in his eyes and he parted the leaves and walked out and stood up, and rising to his feet he was no longer the Saint he had been. And as I watched him go, he was dancing in the chains he couldn't see, all pain gone.

The cave of water was expected to arrive at our coast on Easter Sunday. I had no notion of gadding off under the auspices of a mythical water-fish but I went along to watch. It was said to open its mouth shoreward for half an hour on the appointed day, and there would always be the one person on the beach to walk into it and be carried off. Some saw it as the maw of the sea-spirit, others as a water-chariot of the gods. I wasn't going to risk my skeleton being picked clean and washed up somewhere. The Druids had a service of some sort going on when I arrived. They were waving palms and blowing on small gilt trumpets. It was a braying sound. In the manner of duck-shooters simulating mating cries on little horns they hoped to attract their triple-headed saviour, riding out of the chasm on his golden ass.

Whatever it turned out to be, I couldn't imagine walking blind into any submarine arcana. None of us knew what to expect, despite the books I for one had been reading. On the distant horizon I saw a plume of smoke running very rapidly towards us. A column of water – or rather a round-headed heap like an aqueous bonfire, for the sun caught it, and it was ridged on the surface with currents, which interested me, because they showed enormous power focused there. It spun over the water creating a circle of prickling spray for over twelve yards; its own body not more than eight feet high and six across. At times the currents cleared and it was still in itself, with an inner structure of veins and membranes, some dark purple and others silver and gold, catching the sun like greenhouses and rivers in the distance. Then it went opaque once more with cross-hatching currents flickering like fire. I was waiting for doors to open. The Druids had stopped braying and all was quiet except for the hiss of spray. It had stopped offshore some thirteen or fourteen yards away, and a ridge formed on the water and up to the shingle exactly to my own feet. So I was the one favoured! well, I wasn't going anywhere, voluntarily. Then the ridge parted and rolled outward and down, down so deep the sea parted to its depths and I saw hanging forests and mountains, and cities in the forests, herds of swimming animals and my eye had forgotten distance so that it could see all that there was in the sea. My fascination overcame me and I took a step forward . . .

The whole human underworld lies in this stone
It is called a torture stone
Put it in your mouth it will
Vision hell for you. Rebirth may follow.
You will have been felled as by lightning.
My little finger
Hooks the torture-stone
From your gutted mouth . . .

My friend Ambrosius has a fine voice. I don't think much of his poems. Torture-stone? The waterstone of the wise? I'm not going to publish that . . . I listened to him droning on, and then I was distracted by a noise coming from a gap in the bookshelves to my right. I put my head down. Like a distant muttering of thunder or cavalry. Possibly a ventilation shaft amplifying the shuffling of feet somewhere. Then I caught a
66

glint of silver and for an instant the gap looked like a high narrow aquarium-tank, the pane of glass set back in the shelves, lighted, and full of silvery fish, packed against the glass and moving with a soft snub tapping, signalling to me with their snouts on the glass. I reached my finger in to tap back. It passed through the tank, which was no longer there, and I groped around in the space to see what *was* there. I found the edges of the books, and right at the back some hard substance, oblong, wrapped in paper. As I took it out I had a sudden vision of a granite altar-stone covered with eyes that all shut simultaneously as an appearance like the weaving trunk of an elephant issued through the cavemouth into its sanctum, darkened by the shutting of the eyes. I shook my head violently, and it cleared, and there was Ambrosius' voice still droning in the background, and I held in my hand a sweet, an ordinary paper-wrapped toffee. Relieved, I untwirled the ends and popped it into my mouth. . . . I cannot describe the pain, it was falling through a thundercloud of blood with thick gouts of lightning branding my bare skin and the whole cloud yelled with torture. I revived to feel wetness on my chest and a finger hooking in the bloody snot of my mouth for the torture-stone.

Tipping the library into the river with a bulldozer he shouted out to the autumn that it must read that it had fallen before and would rise again, that what was happening to it now had happened many times before. But the brown river swirled with pages and was silent. He took another library and piled it in the city square by the walls pocked with bullet-holes – look! he said to the empty streets, what happened here has happened before, and here I burn the hopes of ten centuries, they will rise again. Then he bent and put a match to the library. It burnt, the flames turning over the leaves rapidly, the library was reading itself for the first time, breaking out into flaming astonishment as it did so. That brain makes a nice warm glow, he remarked. He dressed slowly in a gorgeous uniform of the last President in the ballroom littered with broken glass. As far as he could tell, he was the last man on earth. He wished he were the last woman, for he esteemed woman more than his own destructive sex.

I was in the warehouse of the Chinese section. An agitated messenger in the usual blue cotton rags thrust an envelope in my hand and watched me with sexy eyes. I read the message. My father has shot himself. No more. I guess he has heard about the Chinese boy. I look on the other side of the page. It tells me that the cartridge went off in my father's hand as he was loading the pistol and blew off the top of his ear-finger. Much relieved, I sat down with the messenger boy and loosened the neck of his uniform. I rubbed my fingertips gently over that most female of genitals, the hollow of a little boy's throat. The next thing I knew I was in the American warehouse among gigantic bales of cotton, the smallest big as a suburban bungalow. Far below I heard Amelia calling. I'm coming, I said, and leapt off the edge. There is no more eloquent genitals than the pouting twin bottom-funnels of Amelia. I closed my eyes and leapt. There was a sharp pain in my hand. I opened my eyes at the rough wooden table, staring ruefully at my shattered finger. My blood sang with the impact of the bullet, and I held out my hand like a lighted torch. The candle flickered and went out, but I could still see the torn cartridge rolling as it tinkled over the stone floor by the light of my bloody finger, my glorious open hand.

The chimp bleeds over the cup. I am bound by my regard for the woman. There is no notice given. I am bound by my regard for her. Honey on the knife-point. My regard. I sit in a sandy room. The sun throws a deep blue shadow in the yellow sand. She makes the spiders. The patient animal bleeds. Cracks run all over the fountain, a nail rusts in the basin. She looks up with the eye of a snail, down with the eye of a roc, she lives in the space between, my regard for her has the dimensions of a Dutch giant, I am bound by it, it is as large as anything I can imagine. Whatever it is or wherever, I meet her. I am content. I am bound by my regard for her.

A game played by anglers with their rods and a chess-board. A game of cards played in the fountain's cool water with wet

68

pieces of slate. A game of football played in the reflector of the radio-telescope. A game of counter-intelligence played among the widowers of fishwives. A pack of Tarots painted on fish-scales: a game of baccarat is played with this pack and as the fortunes of the game change, so do the bodies of the players. The gibbon hands the glass shoe to that countess who removes her tiara'd head and substitutes the gondola of a jellyfish; the pavilion of games is at first the reading room of the B.M., then the lido of the Grand Hotel at Gronsk. A game of squash played inside an ancient pipe-organ with a fossilised roc's egg. A game of billiards played on a golden golf-course. A game of courts-martial played in an ancient judiciary. The old bead-game played by a schoolboy under his bedclothes in the dormitory by the light of an electric torch. Three-dimensional draughts played with tweezers under the microscope. A game of golf played along the flat coping-stones of the merchant banks. A game of chemistry played with lights and decaying cheese in glass vessels. A game of jests played with midday tin spoons and plates in a madhouse. A game of oracles played by counting the segments in the breakfast grapefruit every day.

A woman dancing mandalas
I see loose ends only

Wait and see who she marries

Now she's hunting for ivory shells
And weeping over the last chamber
If I could see where it leads to.
Nothing but loose ends, and such beauty.
She enters her placid feint, and sleeps.

He has to have a woman in his home movies,
It doesn't matter who she is,
What she looks like,
If he photographs a gents there's a girl coming out of it.

The currant bushes lie in shadow.
Waking
Her body behaves in a restless unwise fashion.
The woman is the restless movie-maker.

I have wallowed, I have washed,
The world is flesh and shadow,
Her words too.

With unbecoming slyness the saint
Bids us not enlarge on it.

A manure-can filled with lilies of the valley. The trash of a funeral. The horses begin trotting and I watch the wood of the coffin split into white gashes which sprout flowers. The corpse inside has already become a man of flowers with dahlias for eyes and a daisy-chain across his waistcoat of pansies. The undertakers are smoking cigars and passing fruit, and the reins of the horses are ribbons of all colours. These horses, they begin to change colour too, their ebony lightens to green and the green pimples with buds as they trot along, and the green darkens again and antlers spring from their heads, and fissures run over their haunches and they are mossy trunks and I realise my funeral has stopped and I am watching a flowering space between two trees with a view into a ferny valley running with brooks. I look for the undertakers' assistants and I see two crows flying away into the sky like ragged mackintoshes.

Professor Kleinstadt's eyes are two small flasks full of a morbid blue fluid; it has been drained from the jar of the foetus of the bastard child made on the staircase: it was one of Kleinstadt's stories, a warning to cocky students. He described himself as an educator, but apart from his knowledge of anatomy, he seemed negligible. I listened to the mutterings in his sleep one long train journey we took together, so I knew one of his recurrent fantasies: sliding down the banisters as a little boy, thinking of his father, the briar pipe clenched in the strong teeth, warming and cooling with paternal breath, the banisters pleasantly scorching in his crotch, one and the same, always strong and shining, always there somewhere inside him. I wanted to twist Kleinstadt's lecturing nose so that the world could watch these recurrent pictures, turn the tap that would drain the opaque morbid look and show his thoughts in the transparent flasks.

I saw a large dish garnished let down from heaven, and upon the dish a piece of roast meat, and the meat was of a sudden cut up into pieces for the mouth. I could not see the person who cut the meat up. Then I woke and remembered the man who had been with me. I realised he had gone and I had never seen him in the daylight. I opened the front door and there on the sunny step was a small glass bowl of very clear water with some flowers of gorse floating in it. I had an intuition the water was dew. I was away from my table only a moment but when I came back with a glass of milk I found that the diagrams I had been thinking about were already drawn in great detail. I was only away from my table a moment but when I came back to my table with a glass of water I found that the diagrams I had drawn in greater detail had disappeared from the paper. I felt that the day had not been sunny to begin with, but I couldn't remember if it had been raining or not, and I was frightened that I would not remember this sunshine or whether I was to draw my diagrams today or write some letters.

The accident quite pardonable in a child or a dying person, it happens to me merely because I am concentrating. Scientists and mental nurses are not troubled in this way. Scientists and mental nurses make no attempt to resemble the substances in their laboratories. The scientist: there is a polished globe on his table full of red bromine gas. Me: Oh how I would love to roll in this colour, be impregnated by this gas. But I know that my skin would slough off like a pair of pulpy yellow pyjamas. The strain of restraint – a fart and a little jet. And that little rubber bottle? That is hydrofluoric acid, that eats gold. Oh the beauty! I can't say the words 'autumn tree' without my mouth filling with clear autumn rivers patina'd with rusty leaves thin as eyelids. Watch our faces, the wind peers from them as from the head of a tree. And the accident – fertility and soil! Mental nurses and scientists are all born wearing identical thin clean spectacles from the womb.

The winged thunder will lead me. A kitten bringing home glow-worms instead of mice. A plate of bones and fingernails. Rattling piles of purple mussel-shells. And the crazed wood will decay, shining. In the springshine, the two need only ask. The cave guillotine, the larder guillotine, the dark-room guillotine. The Phantom of the Opera has left his white gloves. Punishment should be followed by something amusing. The birth of the New Year's Bull-Calf from a date cluster. She jumps three times over the fire. The cold houses of the old maids had the shiniest furniture. Fire is cookery and apocalypse. The birds, delightful vases, that sing, parting the atmosphere. A nice brown-and-ginger young gentleman. The clock hammers out a labyrinth. The divine body is the road travelled by the seeker. Each one of you fits my lock. Sayings whispered to me by somebody sitting on the sill of my ear. To whom do these sayings belong?

My father's mother has died. He said nothing about the funeral until I asked. Then he said 'Grief at 4.30 sharp', and started weeping. His face blotched and his nose sharp. There was a loose-leaf printed book on the table, the service-manual of his new car, open at the wiring diagram. It looked like the image of a city, a comity. He made his usual joke: we'll have to change it, the ashtrays are full already. Then his face crumpled and he started weeping again.

I killed the corn-dolly by cutting its sash. The blue woman stood upright in the bowl of the moon. I employed a music-word and the carriage stopped. We were not alone on the snow-plains. I took the goad from its sheath. A fine dry rain started. I saved my silks, tissue-paper tacked over my cuffs. She is part of the minster. A tomb, with the television on. The way of the world. The dance which is also the floor.

A bit of blue sky found in an uncorked bottle of ink, a book with harp-strings instead of words, a rougher, Celtic book with crackling tree-tops instead of words, the mind hums through them, books with print like jagged shadows under an operating light, a row of supple volumes bound in a herd of gazelles, the librarian with a pine-slender face, the sparks clashed from two fighting snails on the windowsill: the egoist sits in the library swollen with the marvels there are in books, the transformations, the civilisations and universes; sitting on the brink of the library and endlessly entertained by hints and glimpses of treasure that he finds in the faces of readers, but alas, the egoist is dyslectic. His word-blindness is absolute. He cannot read at all.

Look unto the rock whence ye are hewn, and to the hole of the pit whence ye are digged. The shadow of the great rock crawled over house and garden, the pit at its foot brimmed with misty shadows. Noon slung its small cape on the rock, and entered the pit, the pebbly soil smelt very good, like tobacco and bread. In the house was a chimney, and a great hearth, on the mantelpiece was a hollow geolite and an oblong pebble. I was given a flask of oil-of-smoke as a keepsake: the essence of the great rock adventures through the vast pit of the air, fire gives the rock wings, and mineral oil its smoky flesh.

Then he mentioned that children do not smile or shed tears until they are forty days old, the light shining in his timeless eyeglasses, as he took my wrist in finger and thumb for my pulse. You must go skating more, he said. I glide pushing the long white floor backwards between the flat lands and the black woods, the wind is behind me going, I hope it will change for me to return. I want skates like butcher's knives, I want easy skates like flatfish, I want skates made of honed bones taken from executed politicians: the speed would taste different. I go back to the doctor and he takes my blood pressure and gives me some purple capsules. There is an old remedy, I thought he said, for your condition. A meal of hairless young mice washed down with cider. I left his consulting-room. I will have those mice, they are blind, they cannot reproach like children's eyes, they cannot smile either, and they cannot eat my heart out from inside for they have no teeth. Outside the doctor's house, I noticed that he had added a trompe l'œil perspective to his garden, on the house wall. Real swallows were alighting on the painted railings. I thought of his spectacles, white like clocks without hands, and decided that I preferred folk-medicine. Was that the book his absent eyes were perusing? Blood and cider! the thought made me shudder, but I felt my cheeks glowing and the air was brisker. I would take each by the tail and tear it with my teeth, like Saturn and his children. I recalled that stately Prince of Cornwall who had cured his leprosy by wallowing with his pigs in their mire.

I was there. The house where the smoke from the chimneys is as red as blood. The woman in the house who is also the floor. Her bodice flows into her skirt, her skirt weaves into the carpet. The old man in the kitchen who is also the oven. The young woman of the house who enters from the drains, wearing green. The young man who visits her smelling of a mown lawn. The meals of appleseeds served. The warm petrol drunk. The stairs that are the keys of a piano that musics them upstairs. The bed that is a silted inlet. The covers that are white and salt and the bedlight that goes down red. The awakening to gulls and sleet. The breakfast of loose change. The street homeward that is a well.

My own stained-glass windows. Saint Septimus choking on a chop. Lady Venus taking a shower in her nightie, or awaiting Hephaistos on a bed of bluebells. The Keystone Cops, with taped sound. The great Rose Window in the North Transept: an impression in stained glass of a bilberry and custard pie in the moment before impact. Mr Maskelyne performing in his Chinese rags. A sequence depicting the gelding of pigs in the month of October. All doors fitted with zip fasteners. No admittance.

A figure seated. A lap in the clothes of a faceless figure. A

74

door in the clothes. The door opens. God has stopped by. The door closes. God has gone, for the moment. Everything's changed. It is now a shell. A shell set in the wall. God's coming back. There goes his white shadow. Now it's a skull. A skull in the wall. The bone is very clean. God draws a curtain so I can see better. The head has been sliced open. I look down into the brain folds, the phlegm of the tissues. The eyes roll at me. The mouth opens and the head begins to speak. It says Waaa Waaa. Yes, I say, yes? Then God opens the door, and closes it again. Just the skull. The thin bone transmits a rosy light. I notice that the door is ajar. I love to come to this living skull, I say, and consider the thin and alive bone surrounded by its arteries and veins embedded in the walls like fossil ferns and embossed roses and the brain nowhere to be seen and the eyes somewhere else and no hands. I love this place, O God. The door opens wide and closes again. O yes God I love coming to this well I love this place God with the little finger of your Mother under a thatch and goodness there's the Lord Jesus drawing water out of the well gouging it up in leather buckets and I step forward to receive his blessing and he tips one of his buckets of water all over me and lifts up the other one and does the same and I am standing sweat-drenched in the haunted house and I wish Jesus was here with me and we were reading books together and he was saying the commandments with me to prove he's not a ghost, but he's not here only me so far and not halfway through the night, but God the haunted house is truly most comfortable with my candle and my stick and my brace of pistols on the mantelpiece and the room with the scorched cradle upstairs. The door is opening slowly.

The door is opening slowly on a church-history lecture. This is how it goes. A white-black statue, a church on end, a muddy well, a quick snoop through the key-hole. That lock's never been used, draperies of dust hang and drag in its halls. The key of the key, books were the key. Living books, the withered old hand tells the painted pictures. The sunshine moves through the stained-glass windows. No one pays attention,

75

since it will resume its task the next day. A living statue, the shadows circulate through its veins. The white statue and the wrong side of the Virgin, where the spiders crouch, apparently doing nothing, in reality digesting the contents of the lists she passes them when I am not looking, with her left hand. The wrong side of the sunshine, the other side of the bird's shout, the space between a woman and her shadow, a distinction lost in the dark bedroom. I will pay someone to go to church for me. The well, the well, it's odd to have the well, the dance-floor at the brink of the well; but they say the resorts are dangerous. I stole something from inside the well when I was in the church. There's a door in the surface, a prayer to go safely through. They learn the tattle there. A chapel shapes the ends, a noble brow, and the stained glass where the sun shines. What do they say. I examine the tall window with binoculars, mind the well! Contented keys to unlock me.

Thus I stand in the unused lock, and the sunshine fades in the West Window. Dark like a key approaches me from the altar. My head reflects through the dark well. I get up and begin to dance. I was angry when they started to write, and I snatched the keys from them. I kept the hell-key, the kiln-key, the key to the key. Each one of you fits my lock. You think I am giving you keys. I am giving you locks. The World has started turning, and the meridians intertwining. The statue descends, singing the great earth mask as it goes. A great head rises gibbering and all goes dark.

Well, lads, I've had my say. Now you know as much about masturbation as I do. Everyone does it. I wonder why I'm blushing. As you wash your lovely faces in the morning, remember a faucet is a little door in the well, and you turn the key and open the door, and let the forceful and graceful creature water in, riding, rising into your world, limpid gibbering. I am living water, boys, in a deep well laid on its side, I am water, boys, and I have just finished dancing for good.

The electricity-bone, the spook-rain, and the tree's one organ, the leaf. Passing the ghost, creating the spook-rain from the power-bone, under the one-organed tree. The spook rains

76

from the ten fingers, the palms of the hands are like boiling silver. Under the organs the ghost-body is created out of the rain coming from the ten fingers and the palm. This is the body that is seen by its skin to crackle upwards, and to crackle downwards. It skirts are ice of electricity and are faintly seen by their own light under the dark organs in the tree-rain. One grain of pollen contains these lovers. Then the bell cleared the school and struck a path through the clouds and left the stone tingling. They were gold-lined, with veins full of frankincense, and there was a child.

II

Soliloquy by the well
The blue sky stretches me out towards it. I lift my hands; they are pulled out like staircase starbeams: I heave them back to my sides, an intolerable tension, then a soundless thunderpeal that rolls round the hills as the beams snap. Leaving them up for long topples me into the blue gulf headlong. I look at the walls of the castle. Immediately I have been standing here for centuries and my weight sinks me into the earth an inch every hundred years. My stone drinks in the rain thirstily. It itches with arrow-grazes. Where is my rest? The Neolithic vase? My escape, the chipped and fissured. I have been standing here four thousand years, on my head, my back passage high in the air and wide open, and everything from pebbles to fresh blood has been poured in it. The new crack is painful as a luminous edge, but is my way out. Where is my rest? A well at the foot of the hill, a well, an estuary silted with slow structure and movement, waterworks and tidal pools, a well, a particular woman, the well of a particular woman.

The June bugs are a splashed armamentarium. Muscular juices the summer distilled and clothed, thirstily drunk up by that same summer's stones. Said the blond man, weeping. The bath had been filled, from its two taps. The sunbeam sits folded in the water. The chemist's shop the same. This was a blasphemy of the teenage vandals. What he separated, dripped and mingled from his shelves. The walking-stick, run as along railings, smashing his rows of substances, his columns of index and purity. I think that any father would inevitably disappoint the gifted imagination of his child. In his laboratory, a wilderness of pipettes and sunlight. Said the blond man, rubbing his boots clean from June bug on the grass verge. The young mothers wheeling past their padded conches with the little scrap of pink meat, nose-in-air. A herd of me on motor-bikes, racing with the summer draggled behind me.

I kneeled down to say my early-morning prayers. The soliloquy was going well. But then I looked down and saw I was casting no shadow. With an apology muttered to God I got up and hurried across to the wardrobe mirror. I cast no reflection. I was not invisible because if I had been transparent it would have been black in my eyes and I would have been blind, with my eyes like glass cameras, unable to take pictures. I checked this by leaning out of the window and waving to the paper-seller, three doors down. He waved back.

It had clearly been something in the prayers I was saying. Our Father . . . perhaps I will say, Our Father-Mother . . . which art in heaven . . . no, I will say, in heaven on earth . . . hallowed be your names, your kingdom come, your will be done in earth as it is in heaven . . . now I saw a little dark stream flicker on the wall in front of me, a darkness turning sideways in the streaming sunlight . . . Give us this day our daily bread, and forgive us our trespasses as we forgive them that trespass against us. For yours is the kingdom the power . . . something had gone very wrong. My shadow, which was gaining strength like smoke from a bonfire of damp wood, suddenly faded, and then blazed so intensely white that I had to throw my hands up in front of my eyes. When I looked again, there was my shape in the wall as if I had been pulled through it, the mark of a slap on dough. Now, how have I gone wrong, I have misunderstood somewhere, I have misunderstood, and nobody is competent to instruct me, I must make my own prayers . . . ah, as soon as I said that, something dark slipped into the room from the mirror and my body-slam mark on the wall slowly filled and smoothed like new. My new shadow is very dark and hard – I pick at its edges and peel it off the wall and roll it up and put it in my pocket, or I can eat it, I can pull it out of the wall inexhaustibly by standing in a bright light and I have made a cloak of it with a red lining and I have cut out a widow's peak and beard and moustachios all of the intensest black, with a red lining.

The silver, fish-tailed dancer of the sand. Nothing emerges from the dream. The sage sits silently, chewing his finger. There are nights and nights, he says. The moonlight slowly penetrates him, he is nearly gone. Quick! I grab an arm, it feels pulpy. Quick! Tell him one of your dreams. So she pulls her lids down and falls asleep and talks in her sleep. Colours flow back into the old freckled body. The eyes open and begin to twinkle. They begin to blaze. The hair over the collar resembles steam escaping under the lid of a pot. The sun shines from the glass skull. I close my eyes, and I lay my hands on my closed eyes against the light, but not before I see her blind face twist towards it and her mouth open wide as if drinking it.

A swarm of bees like a herd of black-and-yellow swine crosses the road. With a sullen roar the air becomes thick with tight-packed circles and triangles. Night-ink sugary with stars pours out of the bathtaps. The gods hold post-chaise in the linear accelerator tonight, a poster states calmly. Einstein will referee, he is linesman-beekeeper. I have come late to a city engaged in a festival of science. Triangles make the night air difficult to breathe. The lights of the boats in the harbour are like brilliant staircases standing steady on the sea.

There was a woman recovering from a brain operation staying with us. They had made a capacious vessel of her head. The wound was lined with silver. The children stood behind her chair playing with their reflections in it. The operation that had taken the lid off her skull had changed her also from a man into a woman. She had abrupt mood-changes. Sometimes money in her hand changed to fish from sheer joy. Sometimes to soot. And sometimes to more money. She did

79

not sleep well. I used to wake up and hear her in the bathroom: she was sluicing cold water round and round in her head, nodding it out.

One night I heard her get up, and was concerned because there was no further sound. I discovered her in the front garden, silently filling her head with the full moonlight.

He opens the wardrobe. He opens the moonlight. White mist, a view through pouting rain of a meadow without trees. A herd of sheep, crouching draggled under the rain. The view dips its shaggy eyebrows, and the sheep are nearer. They fill the picture and we pass into them. The black slowly lightens and we see a row of hanging woollen suits. He walks forward to take down one of these old suits. It is sopping wet.

'An old dream striped with violence . . .' I wake up with my feet smarting, as if I had been firewalking again. I inspected them: the hard skin was charred. The sheets were streaked with charcoal. This did not mean I was losing. Firewalking is a holy practice. I have never lost in a dream – yet. I have been a patient, I crawled along the asylum parapet, the Doctor shouted at me from the white-painted window, I fell, but I woke before the ground struck. I once woke up during my coronation. My crown was on, my sceptre in my right hand. The metal was gold, but the gems were night-coloured anthracite. I was also wearing pyjamas, up at the high altar of the great cathedral, in front of the sea of ermine capes and coronets, those duchesses, watery with jewels. Oil from the anointing had run into my collar, fragrant and sticky.

Another morning she shouted in my ear, 'Peter! the blood!' I leapt to the present from a dream of decapitation. It was the Boxer risings, I was palace executioner, my axe was doubleheaded, it bit deep, I had honed it all night in the light of the forge-fire.

Once we woke in bed with the miraculous draught of fish. I brought the Holy Grail to England. It is a small battered wooden cup. I have Dracula's cloak and a mahogany box of his ashes, greenish and with his teeth mixed in. Strong white teeth like a cat's. I hope one night to visit an alchemist's. I will

80

snatch the Stone, and mount it in my ring, and then my finger will open a certain corridor between the two worlds, and I shall come and go as I please.

An empty mirror filling up slowly with a black hieroglyph. The neatly-shaved poodle parades the green close lawns: a piece of wiry writing. Black snow falls. Little black footprints run over the clean washing. Ants write a ravenous sentence in the picnic garden. The spider hitches her web about her on the syllable 'snaaaaa' with a silent rattling. The fly completes with a fat little 'aaatch' like a black peach. The mirror empties gradually, then fills up with a white hieroglyph. White poodle, white snow, footmarks invisible on white washing, a dairy spider and a floury fly, a white peach with a brown pinch-mark.

The sorcerer's secretary takes down the spell in rapid short-hand, tears off the page and launches it down the corridor.

This dove flies to the industrialist's breakfast-table with deckle-edged wings and props its invitation against the mar-malade.

The sorcerer wipes his labia on the goldfish he tosses back into the loo-water; it swims sideways and into my shaving-water, and in a voice like the piping of bats invites me to dine.

A white water-spout handles the invitations to the ballet-master and his mistress; it arrives at their ranch invisible due to a dry journey over the steppes; and it replenishes itself with whiteness from the still water in the rain-butt outside on the stoep. The letters of the invitation appear in a row under the everted rim of the spout, under its rim of eyes, under its wide-open shout.

It is now the Christmas tree hung with saints' relics.

I am hung with many microscope lenses; they are a salt day-sweat scrutinising my skin, roving inspectors.

I joined the two luminaries in marriage and we all became as water having two lights.

I am distilling blood of the horse with eight legs, in the sacred bucranium; the figure has a halo of flickering light, like the burning of a city at night.

The cast-up seaweed is tied together in bows from the involved currents; he knocked a spirit-chair together from old packing-cases.

Even the shadows of the wires had gone; the book hummed with the power in it, the letters moved like piston-shafts across the page, the illustrations were steady flashes of lightning.

The dance of the fine gusts of the spider between the flower-stems.

My dead brother gathered full-blown primroses and an armful of brown potatoes in the moonlight; part one of the clock, the bellman cried, and a dry morning, worn thin and frosty.

Later the trees emerged in bud and stood like full glasses of smoky claret; Orion appeared upside-down in her glass of water.

He asked her to go into the wood and tell him what she saw there.

She walked between the trees and the first thing she noticed was a pond.

She knelt down and stripped off the thin skin of reflections, rolled it up and put it in her pocket to show she had been there.

The water's new skin reflected with more brilliance and better colour.

So she knelt down and took this new skin and put it in her pocket, throwing the other skin away.

But the colours of the newest skin were without equal, so she took this instead.

In due time she emptied the pond in this manner.

There was a hole in the ground, a quag with a few fish slapping about in it; she felt sorry for the fish so she took off her shoes and went down into the quagmire: it came up to her knees. She captured the fish and put them in her skirt and climbed out.

She found where the torn scraps of reflection had settled among the trees, and she slid a fish into each one.

Then she went back to him. What is that wet patch on your

skirt? were his first words . . . but his suspicions were drowned in amazement when she unrolled the tapestry of colours for him.

I sent her into the wineglass to listen.

I prodded her into the apple-barrow; I told her to take out her pin-dagger as soon as she heard the maggot chewing.

I gave her a bath in a walnut-shell.

She made a salt necklace, piercing the crystals together.

I was frightened when she fell in the mustard, but I rolled her clean on a piece of bread.

I told her to sit in the cruet like an information kiosk and answer my questions.

I compiled a savoury blanc-mange for her studded with angelica; it was a gobbet of my fish-sauce.

But she ran from the reek of my steak, the evisceration of an elephant; I gave her a cress-leaf fan.

She got drunk in a grape. I found her snoring like a fly on her back in the punctured skin.

It was after I had eaten the blood-orange that I missed her.

I was about to wipe my mouth on the spotted handkerchief when I saw the spotted butterfly; reaching for it I noticed an auburn-spotted hemlock, warm in the sun and rank with its hanging vapours; but then a polka-dotted dalmatian dog ran past and I went up to the owner, but as I started to ask his permission my eye travelled downwards and I noticed he was wearing a dotted shirt, excuse me I said . . . but then the nurse hurried past, the one with the spotty face. I followed close on her heels but then I noticed a newspaper on a bench: the small print and the grainy photographs fascinated me and the swarms of letters gave me the library idea so I turned to go there but a beam of sunlight struck down into the stream by the road and picked out the rosy-dotted side of a neat fish swimming in one place against the current so I leapt in on top of this. The spotty nurse, seeing my danger, was kind enough to jump in after me and the sight of the great dot of her nipple through the wet nylon uniform reminded me of my purpose so treading water I bent forward to take it in my mouth but before I could make contact she knocked me out and towed me ashore.

Somebody clouted his head and he shuddered into many ghosts.

The one that stayed behind was too unhappy, it condensed into a dung-beetle.

Here! cried the back-passage of the cadaver.

Wincing along it went the beetle, pincers busy.

And indeed it was delicious, eating himself.

And as he mounted he met and digested many troubles, and was a brass beetle that turned itself by further eating into a silver beetle, for he met the joys and munched them. He was among the information now but it did him no good, he spat it out like borage.

Then he desired light, sawing a hole in the skull, and he stepped over the sill into the sunlight, a gold beetle that spread its wings and flew away to the midden, and to the log.

A little bloodstained clockwork in a puddle of blood.

She picked it up sighing, wiped it on her skirt.

Look, she said, it's all that's left of Silas, I wonder what could have done it?

I shrugged my heavy shoulders.

I don't know, she said, whether one can give a piece of machinery a proper burial. Might it not be better, she sniggered, to fasten it in a memorial clock, so one always thought of poor Silas when one looked at the time?

My eye itched, I rubbed it on my flank.

I suppose he was thrown from his elephant, she said, placing one tiny foot in the crook of my trunk, and when they dragged him away this piece remained.

I hoisted her to my back.

But I don't want the beastly thing, she cried from the howdah, and she flung the clockwork into the swamp.

As we left, I saw it turning into a golden beetle.

Among our other equipment we had a portable cave, canvas and struts, painted to look like rocks.

An oil lamp to throw out a mysterious gleam.

Gipsy clothes and an ageing wig with its own face-wrinkles and a pipe attached for her; so long as the pipe was held in the teeth they were black and therefore invisible.

A pipe is a portable altar.

It is the entranceway of Pimlico Electricals Ltd; the lights are off; the commissionaire has gone home; street-lamps hoist lanky shadows.

Under her direction I grow thin enough to handle the equipment: I set our cave up against the entrance of the steel-and-glass building, and its light beckons the moths.

The first to arrive is a policeman, who cannot believe his eyes, his wireless whispering over his left breast; he squares his shoulders and marches in; after this we catch a cab-driver, three late theatre-goers, and a mother hurrying past whose three children see us and pull her up short.

At the first breath of dawn we pack the cave together and stow it back in the howdah. I have no idea what happens to the visitors, and I never mention the subject. I expect they learn something. They may ascend to a better life on the ladder of her pipe-smoke.

Before I was her draught-animal, before she died, she was always trying to frighten me. My heart breaks, I should have loved her better. Now we are automatic, a symbiosis. I will make myself smaller.

At that time, I might walk into the bedroom and find a giant fingerstall motionless on the floor. Then it would begin to loop along, like a caterpillar, and a muffled cackling coming from inside – my spouse!

She once appeared at the top of the stairs looking like a spiritualist's photograph, with a piece of cheese-cloth over her. She gave me a box of foaming blood capsules on my birthday.

Then she had to go into hospital. Her letters were always recalling 'Do you remember when I . . .'

Are always recalling. Her voice lives along those lines.

Her jokes turned out to be true. Prophetic of what was going to happen to her. At first her spirit only visited me in these letters.

Now it drives me about the streets. As she takes the great goad from its sheath it crackles with lightning.

If only I'd ripped off the chrysalis-sheet, or covered the cheese-cloth with bloody kisses, she would have lived in the body, she would not have towered over me like this. I have been her boat and its oars and the multitude that rowed her. A quadrillion curse, and she the man in the boat. She would lie back on the bed with her legs wide in front of the mirror, and her finger would raise the man, and we'd all go rowing, faster and heavier, and great clods of sea would come up with our oars, and we'd be a herd of elephant stampeding with great ears, and we'd all disappear suddenly and only the plain heaving with our thunder, all gone but me, and she'd walk insolently up to me and put her tiny foot in the crook of my trunk.

III

The Mirror passage
The mirror-passage beaming an aura of perfection.

That's where I lost my arm.

The bearings are so smooth you cannot feel vibration.

When it slowed down, constellations appeared in it, and a fine white scum accumulated on the floor beneath it, through it I saw mountains and turf and a herd of ponies running, their heads all turning at once.

Then the machine disappeared and I was in the world I now inhabit, my arm restored.

But then I was in two places at once: soaping my breasts in the warm water; impatiently gelding the pigs.

The circles are conscious of the skirt, the dot is a conscious place in that white magnitude. The snailshell is a circledot smacked sideways, issuing upwards, growing smaller. This is the explanation of Beethoven on discs.

Smoke does not find definition tedious: it is a faster medium, like clouds. Everything echoes. Bird-cries bruise the underclouds and the upperleaves. Rocks are the slow echo.

86

The stone parapet watches the burning city.
The temple hoards its idols on wide shelves.
Spectra shift on towards the red.
Now I begin to remember the evening.
A flame-coloured skirt. Is she still wearing it?
I take down tragic books full of burning.
She must not wear that choker so broad.

I grasp the difficult mathematics of topology because I know her saddle-shapes, I know conic sections from the fall of her skirt, transcendental numbers are not difficult since inside she is much bigger than she is outside, and as for theology, she always gives me good answers. Am I learned then, or is she? Neither, but we fit, and her flame-coloured skirt haunts my pages, and I live there too. Her friends say I sometimes look out of her eyes.

IV

Music and leaves

Music, leaves, a lake, and the city beside the mound.

A suitcase, a pass, Blake's works, and a painful tooth.

A uniform, a death-warrant, the priest protests, he strikes the condemned man.

The coloured man's invention, a green milk-shake, the lawyer's brief, a dentist's chair.

The bruise fades from purple to russet, a slap shaped like a laurel-leaf, salt toes, a lizard-burrow at the foot of the cliff.

She sits at her wish-table counting out metal wheat.

He turns a screw, the apparatus of rods and mirrors starts spinning.

Where is she? The bottom of my glass rises towards me. I grow smaller as I hurtle towards it so that I shall never strike the glass.

Is she here? The lump of ore falls out of the knapsack.

Or here? A window with a garden painted on it.

A wishing well with a thatch, waterless.

The veins in the stone begin beating.

All stones are lucky; sand-grains are fortunate, mountains are holy.

A wish-table and she is counting out knives.

I close my eyes: the inside of the lids is painted with a garden.

She is picking delphiniums. She is selecting honeys.

I open my eyes, she is counting ... 149, 150 ... and tries the one-hundred and fiftieth dagger-blade against her soft cheek.

I close my eyes.

A garden. The veins in the garden begin to beat.

v

Now she steps into the chancel

Immediately I am among gesticulating figures rinsing sacred vessels, dropping curtseys ahead of them. They are all men, but they are wearing black dresses like mine.

I decide to watch the show from the nave, and open one of the numerous small books giving the order of service.

In no time at all I am bobbing, crossing myself, and apologising for being a woman.

This is no good, say I, snapping the book shut and shouting to the priests who are fiddling with a little dish covered with a white cloth. They turn their pale faces and look at me.

Before they can look away I lift up my skirt. Then I start tickling myself. The wooden beams crack and a lump of masonry falls on the altar. I tickle myself harder.

The church fades away. A holidaymaker I recognise as one of the priests got up in shirtsleeves and coloured scarf sidles through the tentflap.

Cross my palm with silver wheat, I say. Shall I tell him what will happen, or what he wishes for himself? The two will not be so very different, since I am the fortune-teller. So I tell him what I wish for myself. And a new religion is born.

Mud-feelings
A matter of opening pathways, he thought.

True, she said, I'd like to hear more about that.

Well, he said, that brown sugar you were eating in your dream . . .

No! she said, that's horrid.

That's why your dream made it brown *sugar*.

Well, she said, I cut it up into four equal slices.

It's the same stuff, however many slices you cut it up into, he pointed out.

That's true, she said.

Well, then, he said, there's a path open. When I sat you down in the mud in your white dress, you said it made you feel like a goddess.

I was surprised, she said. If we'd gone on we would have been completely alike, two clay figures. It erased the difference. Afterwards we would have known what it felt like to be the other. So it's a path. I think we're as full of paths as veined marble, she declared.

I am the statue, he said, and I begin to breathe.

VII

And triangles
There's no such thing. A triangle is an abstraction, a word, a slice, the mark of wind on water.

What is it a slice of? she asked.

And that's another thing, he went on. Not only is a triangle a nothing. One triangle is less than nothing. A triangle only begins to have meaning as one of a pair.

That makes sense, she said.

So, he resumed, a triangle is a slice of a cave or a snail's shell or a whirlwind or a volcano (that geological maelstrom) a womb or a penis or a lily.

I thought it would come to that, she said.

I refuse to be distracted; none of these things acts on its own behalf. The whirlwind ransacks the land, the cave shelters the spring, the volcano teaches the sky thunder. When the one acts, the other attends; when the one is emptying the other is filling; when the one is light, the other is dark and shadows of light growl in it, streaks of dawn; and when the one is female the other is male, and the male never rests until he becomes female nor the female until she has become male.

Here are some ribbons for your hair, she said.

Thank you, he said humbly.

VIII

Microscale
Eggs reflected in a fat mirror.

Open the female bible and be saved.

X-ray the book; its radiograph resembles that of the snake; a winding spiral.

The snake creates its own etched plate for printing by falling on the hotplate: the shrivelling snakeflesh bites deep into the metal.

Baby's tears pull the wife's face off and let it go with a snap, it resettles like crumpled elastic.

A two-ounce wash-leather bag of diatomaceous dust: I puff a pinch of it in the air and the furniture is covered with a thin innumerable layer of consummate sculpture in a tough silica.

The microscope is the prick of a man interested in inward things.

Smoke is spiny swarms.

The electricity in a baby's tears attracts dust in flocks.

Dust settles on the mirrors, it is ragged dust, it weaves itself into sheets inside the mirrors.

The eggs are not fat enough; they hatch in the mirrors but not outside.

I put my ear to the frame and listen to the cheeping.

The baby settles inside the mirror and will not be dislodged. You can see his small frightened face peering out still, though the family moved away two years ago.

The wife's face doesn't fit any more; she grows wrinkles like the radiograph of the snake. She is two years away.

Like the microscope, I am interested in the innumerable masterpieces.

I save my bible, bound in my mother's skin, from the fire.

A masterpiece bound in tough silence.

A door in the flower.

I break a spiral staircase out of the peascod.

There is a chandelier in a ballroom in a palace in the stone head of this idol. At present it is dark.

I bring a bowl of warm blood and lay it on the knees.

Inside, one couple dances in the blood-red dawn.

I bring an egg and crack it over the head. The yolk runs down. The sun rises inside.

I bring milk and dash it in the stone face. Dawn mists stalk the palace avenues.

I resume sculpting the hand. A landau drives up, a tall muslin lady alights at the front door.

I light the bonfire. The Captain of Horse greets the beautiful lady.

I set the barbarous idol in the centre of the fire's red socket. Their liaison is consummated in the royal bed.

I set wine in front of the cooling figure. Inside, a sunset like oil and blood and a night like the interior of a grape, sweet and ripe. A seed in a lady at the centre of a night at the centre of the head of a half-finished stone idol that has been splashed with milk, egg and blood and roasted in the fire.

IX

Some of her dimensions
In the first place, she has six-dimensional laughter.

Then her face closes placidly on twelve horizons intersecting at right angles.

She dresses in colours that taste of wells.

She stands on pebbled beaches, and history is the skulls of foes.

She stands on sandy beaches, and history has no room for mankind.

She builds a sandcastle with bucket and spade, and this creates a tide of children.

She paddles and the tide inches up her legs. Immediately I contain the sea and bring it to her in my arms. I am full of seaweed and ink. My brine wets her skirts with a quick facetious splash that makes her laugh. But I travel through her vesture.

She walks slowly along my shore.

My surface shines with a straight path that reaches like a pang as far as the setting sun.

Then only lips remained, calling feebly for their mother.

The hand still gripped the handkerchief. It went on feebly polishing the spokes of the steel bridge.

Blood swallows the peasant's hut.

The brains float away with the sun shining through them.

The bones collapse like a staircase of steel rods.

The eyes look wise and drop one greasy tear with great deliberation.

The penis waddles on to the rocky promontory, and the explosion has turned it black.

It hops onto the rim of the birdbath and grins with its severed part on scenting that it is still full of milk.

Children, children! she said, and placed all the pieces she could find into a hamper.

The naughty black penis bird she shut up into a pebble.

She told the pieces in the hamper both nice and nasty stories until they began to walk about and became the people we know now.

That lady was my ancestress.

I myself was walking on the sea-shore when I heard a long high-pitched whistle on two notes.

It stopped suddenly, and a bearded man walked out from

behind a large rock.

This large man. I loved myself first, now I love him. He loved me.

Tired out by love, we were fond of riffling through great books, encyclopaedias. He was systematic, I darted in and out of the books.

I saw him lose his temper only once. He had got as far as the S-T volume. The article called REGENERATION.

'Look,' he said, 'this picture of the frog growing a new leg. Very fine. But the text says that the leg will simply die. The severed leg, unlike the raw hip-joint, lacks the wisdom to grow a new frog. It must have been discouraged by the mournful atmosphere of the laboratory.'

Such a beautiful man! but so strange. Parts of him were as white as something that had spent its whole life in a cave. Almost transparent, like porcelain. But his genitals were inky black, like warm night coming into me.

His chest was set with one of these pale windows, and when he was in a calm mood you could see his heart, like a great plum, pulsating on a trellis. Startle him, a shout as he was reading, and the fruit disappeared in a swarm of blood-vessels.

His flesh was like a warm veined marble with windows and corridors in it, with this great inky member at his crotch hanging like a fall of night, or striking out, luminously black, showing the thud of blood in it.

His seed was not pale, like that of other men, or like seed grown in a dark cave – it was brilliantly yellow, like pollen, or a beam of sunlight.

He never talked about family, his or mine, except for this tale he told me about my ancestress, and how he grew like an embryo from his penis, ripped out and black with the explosion she made.

x

Her waking thoughts
The creation of a globe of knots instead of a moon.

But the moon still rides over the sea tying and untying knots in the tides, which is why they are called 'tied'.

The shark learnt mutilation from the render of the tree and the maker of applewood coffins. No fish travelled with Noah, no fish had the baptism of the flood for they breathe water, no fish changes its skin or winks.

What horror under the black cloth on the dresser? The full Moon!

Overthrowing those skins which should chime together like men and women singing, this is how the mantra affrights. There is the root and the root mark, chewing the diamond.

Small tears singing praise follow the pearl, a rainbow plays on the bathroom tiles. If playing strong virgin won't work, bite off your lip.

Blondes and then sand.

The track of white hands led across the desert.

His head was a glass of water. He smiled slowly, and the glass split.

All this cancelling of glass, I would have it flow to the bottom of the sea, it might do what it wanted there.

I was present at the creation of the octahedron in the globe, the yacht in the breeze, the lady with the glass-marble child.

An hour-glass full of wax, for the summer months. How the sun fills the air spaces with doorways.

Grandmother's will was against me, but they lent me Samuel's Rolls Royce to go home in. She left the money to a great many strange persons, to fit out a library in the family chapel. Rose asked me whether I would take it to a higher court. I replied that that was just words, nobody got out scot-free.

Meanwhile the thin blades crackle through the sealed flaps of begging letters.

XI

An outsider's view of the professor
The earth's liquid core acts like a dynamo, said Professor

James. Look!

He touched me and my hair crinkled like a negro's.

He snapped his fingers and long sparks shot out.

I saw he was walking sideways and his shirt was not linen, it was electricity, with a jagged flash at his laughing throat.

It would blacken you to sleep with me, he called; and as he came closer my clothes streamed in a wind.

But before he touched me a sudden realisation came over his face, a sudden change. His expression crumbled like soil over his face, his face crumbled like soil over rock, rock crumbled like soil in his face, a volcano erupted with teeth. Amen! his voice came. Halleluja! Now it was food coming thick and fast.

The landscapes he had seen were coming through his skin. The food he had eaten was coming through his skin. Now he was smaller. Preparing for his first meal and his first sight of outdoors.

As he stepped through the front of his jacket he held his hands up to me and called out 'Mother?'

But I am the mother of sharks and electricity and he had disqualified.

I said to him: watch the stars, watch your making. The worm, slime-gowned on the path between the oak-trees, watches the stars roll through the cylindrical lens of its whole body. It is content. The church, a stationary spread of cards, watches the stars making the men that will not tend it. I watch my genitals make my husband's child. The nurses tear at the caul smothering his features with muslin. He looks like a spiritualist's photograph. The baby brays with rage. Under the stars my husband spattered me with oak-sperm, he pelted me with acorns.

I have a boat that is always favoured with a correct wind.

There is a man in that boat who rows my way always.

I have a purse with a coin in it. Spend that coin, and another takes its place.

There is an ear I know, the ear of a horse I ride. If I am

95

hungry or thirsty and I whisper of my need into that ear the satisfaction of my need will be forthcoming.

There is a witty head with saliva in its beard that is my constant companion.

This head will joke with me and give me liquor so that I am mad with delight and cannot tell the time.

There is a hall I know and I know the opening of the door of it, and in that hall there are always lights, and a banquet. The feasting men turn to me as I enter and I am one of them immediately.

Or it is a church, and they will divide my flesh and eat and drink of me.

Or it is a theatre with scene changing to scene and a company of interesting people unknown to me as the lights go up, it is a drive through my own lands of which I am queen, and it is a boat that always has a favouring wind, and a sewer with rats in it for my enemies.

I travelled through Cornwall with the new atlas of mines, searching for the egg in the red nest.

I glazed a window in its shell and peered into its interior.

The yolk was a striated cube, like a chest of three-dimensional sigils, or computer circuits.

I swung the sword to murder the egg. The rebound would have severed my head, but I ducked and it took a lock of hair.

I noosed my hair and cut into the egg with ease. The golden cube rocked on the amber white. My silver ladle dug. I didn't care what pangs the broken circuits felt.

The city tasted long Emily and snowing upwards or down in the mouth (that was the pangs) and like a slippery map. I gave up its unpained gross and walked in it, though pavement tasted too bad and the door with the brass screws. No adjustments were now possible, the eyepaths were drilled down to the taste-lobes. The horse was crunchy and too large to bite. I was hungry and so was the glossy shit-coil, very chestnut, but I won. The slice of moon was large too but the white juice was nice. I licked the church and the sun-pollen on its windows. The priest tasted the same but the congregation tasted of rage hiding in rags. This told me that hell was built with bricks of silence.

Gun barrels glint, gathered in mineral ambush.

The plan of a city engraved on the skeleton of a leaf.

The scale is enlarged as the traveller approaches the better-known places.

The church in the sunlight looks like a red frog in a yellow tree.

The sealed chancel is lined with red plush. There is a sealed casket in this chancel resting in the palm of an iron gauntlet lying on the altar.

In the casket there is a white book and a bullet floating on quicksilver.

There are drunken angels on guard in the sky. They resemble tall thin glasses of brandy almost invisible in the amber twilight.

Now the day is going I can see that where her dress laps, dazzling light pours from the folds.

She tells me how she began by studying singing for her health, and that she sang this landscape, but now she was studying its secrets.

As the leaves drop, she wonders about the bullet, and believes that it has been fired. It passed through a heart, and this is the reason for the casket, and for the church.

The white book records her song in succinct black diagrams. The mailed fist crushes the casket if she guesses too soon and wrongly.

The quicksilver is a loving and ignorant heart learning the book and the bullet, and digesting them.

Then it will digest the church, and it will look like itself, a quivering mirror, to her, but like a man to other men.

The other church was a lion three miles long. The altar was a closed room without windows. Four martyrs sat in this room.

The cloth shone, lulled. Then the lion opened his eyes and all rooms lighted, including the sealed altar. The martyrs raised their cups to drink.

97

Then the lion closed his eyes. The martyrs' cups are still raised, undrunk.

Then the lion opened his jaws, to swallow the sun's apricot juices. At this moment the congregation entered.

The congregation took no acount of jaws, only in the times of evening service, which were synchronised to the opening of the jaws.

Then the lion got up and walked away from the church. The congregation did not notice this happen. I saw it go, and so did she. The martyrs are still unable to quaff their cups; this needs the presence of the lion.

The next time I noticed the lion it entered our bedroom and lay down with us. It entered with its mouth open because the sun was shining. She and I were able to toast each other with a love potion because the lion was shining with open mouth. Our wishes and doings correspond with those of the lion, and we hope it will always be so.

The steady flow of shafts from the capitals to the springing of the vaults and the huge verticals which stream unbroken from vault to floor remind the spectator of the ancient saying: as above, so below. This was his remark aloud.

To her he said; old whale's bones, and in the North transept sex opened and shut like a great flapping eyelid over the sun's eye, while he found the triangle at his throat cool with the relaxation of his clothing which extended downwards to his penis-root, and maintained itself like a current.

You shouldn't wear an open-neck shirt in church, she said.

I wanted to bed you down at the navel of the building, he said afterwards, and I'm sure God would have liked it watching from the ceiling, watching from the floor. Now the architecture seems feminine, in tubes, cornets and conches.

The raven rowing home.

The sparks of sun understanding their last half-hour.

The day-scents have switched off, the night-scents have not yet begun to bleed.

There is a half-dead feeling about the face, the sandy stone sings in its grains, each to each, there is an elastic strain gathering in the sky, and there is peaceful catastrophe of blood and cider wreckage in the west.

There is an interval during which books open and are fallen into, snacks and meals diffuse their switchgear through the flesh, turning this off and that on. And finally the descent backwards into the skull.

The early riser pulls himself off the bank. The river hums swiftly through crisp grass.

Her window exists, from across the street.

The glass is misted, the curtain lags as though it were hung up wet.

The perfumed twilight is the silk shapes scattered in it.

The small whistle of breathing in the bed.

The slipping into bed. The first touch, a mixture of welcome and astonishment.

Mother says no.

Greta murmuring through the small east window.

The little piscina uninjured and very very old.

All god in a creamy drift of cowslips.

The feast of the transfiguration . . . in whom I am well pleased . . .

And the season passes, girls will be girls, and the absurdity barrier is soon passed.

I must back to my studies.

Embryology is taxing, when Cleopatra holds the shears.

No, my dear Cardinal, allow me.

A grief-stricken cry arises from the milk.

His voice breaks bones, and from the wound the smell of fresh strawberries comes.

The small boy of the house takes bites from pebbles as if they were bread-rolls, his nappy is full of sand.

The little girl turns herself into various flowers, she does this by standing behind them and turning through three right angles; by this means she enters the corridor of the flower.

It is like a green close-set avenue she walks down in the fresh smell of the sap towards a violet light ahead, or a yellow light.

She must not walk right to the end of the avenue, up into the flower, because a grain of pollen or a bee or some other process raving with summer air might point its sword at her, or tie her to the pistil for the monster breeze, the billow of air packed with furious working faces, bearded and shining with oils.

The offspring will be a child feeding on earth and stones like a flower, who drinks the air and water.

The avenue slopes downhill into the hollyhock, it is more and more difficult to keep her footing, the hooded bowl of blue with one answer and one wall opening out with flounces . . . it is too much.

The milk the child needs is blue-veined marble.

XII

The virgin twist

Caught in a trap-bed and a male whore in the Inn of the Copper Snake.

A diabolical black prince beckoning from a contraceptive like the business end of a fairground. The lights flash and the score is marked out on the ceiling.

He rang up X such and suches in this and that time when he noticed his father watching. I didn't want a lesbian wife.

You slut, they said. I ought to skin you.

A little drop of milk fluid splashed from the inn-sign. The snake's jaws were opening slowly. Greasy venom gathered on its pointed teeth.

Tutor of small boys, it eased through the open upper window.

The wind in the solar room bounces from mirror to mirror, scorches.

My sweat feathers from wrist to brow, from chest to knee. I am bound in a garment of it, which rustles.

It is made of red copper.

The blood in my eyes forests and in every drop a bell is tolling.

Soft glass breaks and gives me a skull of ice. There is a sudden picture of a daffodil garden with stone walks and statues that stir.

Now I step out of the shower, very alive, in every crevice clean, like a bed newly made and warmed dry with hasped pans of glowing coals.

Thinking about her presents me with two tiny bouquets of roses that glow through the bosom of my clean white shirt.

The howl that tries to be holy. The bubble won't burst.

It sticks behind the nose and howling is nasal.

Blood-strands, or gum spun off the ventricles, muscles of cobweb?

Still the howl was not holy. He told her the problem.

They made love holy, one finger of hers in his mud.

XIII

The table of manifestation

Three pairs of hands appear. Hands only.

One plays the violin, another lights the candles, the third adjusts my cravat.

She arrives in a straight dress of white silk.

She praises my servants: admires the music, the service, the valeting.

I clap my hands. The meal is served.

One carries in the meat, the second whets the knife, the third carves.

A cycle of sonatas on the piano commences. The meal completes itself, in great harmony.

The first brings in a little table, the second settles us in chairs, the third carries a wand and taps the table.

At the first tap the black wood turns brown, at the second green, and at the third grass prickles through. A little lawn on the table top, smooth as a billiard-table.

A stream creeps across from left to right, crystal-clear and gently purling.

A trapdoor opens and a gold-sheeted bed set in an arbour of

roses rises gently into view.

The wand descends again and traces out a second trapdoor in the turf. It opens and a dazzling light pours forth.

Out of the light step up two figures, hand in hand. They make their way to the bed.

Lying on the bed they slowly remove each other's clothes. Their faces are replicas of our own. She spills her coffee, which traces an ugly trapdoor on her skirt. She struggles to rise, but the hands prevent us.

I feel a moisture in my groin, the curled stain in her lap shines black. We are compelled to watch.

The small figures arrange themselves. They are wailing monkey embracing a tree, and they come with tiny soprano cries.

They become the bamboo altar, the muscles flower, the Spanish festoon, precession of the gills, in rapid succession I see at the corner of my eye white-gloved fingers keeping her eyes open.

Suddenly the table vanishes and all is dark except for dawn seeping around the curtains.

XIV

These heavy stones
Dirtying ladies' white dresses pleases this boy.

He mingles in crowds with a fountain-pen, he fills a pocket with soot and distributes it with gloved fingers. At parties he is careless with red wine.

Exquisite scenes!

One night on the river boat, a woman new to him sweeps in. A magnificent white gown exposes bird-white shoulders. Something passes between their glances which seemed to understand. They leave together.

There is a mud-bank offshore, stretching under the starry night like a black bed for such lovers as he imagines. They kiss on the riverbank.

To his joy she steps down on the mud. He follows, sinking

to his knees. She walks ahead without soiling a shoe.

He struggles. She turns back. He hears a whisper of skirts and smells a perfume like cut grass-roots. He looks up at her white face bending towards him. She carries a heaviness in her hands. He holds out his and she puts something in them which pushes him backwards with its weight.

He feels the back of his head enter the mud. Mud rolls to his ears and fills them with noisy deafness. The stone he holds presses down on his face. He tries to call out. A picture flashes into his head of a white maggot dug out of black stinking cheese.

In desperation he sinks his teeth into the stone. It is soft like mushroom and melts away in his mouth. He is rising through the stone by drinking it and he finds purchase beneath him, elbowing out of the muck which is now bright with moonlight.

A toad with blue eyes waits under the glass case.

She hands him the keys to the fluoroscope.

Leviathan hides his face behind little stringy hands.

It is the demonstration of the centre of the city by means of an earth-shaking fight. The doctors are powerless. A monument will pass through the hearts of the antagonists.

Hidden in a stinking dust the fight rages through the tenements.

Depressions hired out by the hour. An anonymous detractor dingies all. A flannel on the line bobs through the window and I wheel suddenly. My heart relaxes and the dust goes on falling, greasy pellicle.

Then a convulsion from nowhere rends the skin and the chrysalis splits audibly. The five correct dimensions appear.

More expensive depressions are called the Bell Jar. The world is painted over the inside of a small hollow.

Pills for depression resemble ventriloquists' dummies. The small virile heads speak inside you.

This is an involuntary expense to some person unknown, with no apparent object, hired from invisible shops. The dust twitches, like cogs engaging. Then we have electricity passing, fast and vivid; the depression's fee has expired.

I see a broken face among the tree-roots. A green negro.

The summer lays the beams of its chambers in the waves.

More water stands above the mountains. It is a Medusa the size of England.

This happens while we are still beating the wood for sopranos.

Now he holds up the proud Colonel's severed head, blood spurting from the seven estuaries.

A warm summer wind blows a hole into the glacier, a brightly-coloured parrot flutters out and steps proudly down over the ice-terraces.

With his awl, he pulls himself out into the moonlight.

However I tune myself messages still flashed through mud-puddles, legs, the headlines and Orion's belt.

Here, the jellies are crested, the biscuits bear their coat of arms, and the beer wears a high crown.

I would save myself, I would wear her glasses. It was like looking through long transparent bolts of twisted silk. The ceiling rumbled with stars.

I prime the cannon with bread and milk. My ships tunnel underground. We skim mating over the sea. It shines like plates of crumpled tinfoil.

The waves give birth to themselves, over and over.

I see hanging in the air to left and right of me, keeping up with me, two small green landscapes.

The doctor's pocketbook draws up on the correct platform to keep him in cravats. The little boy swears at the soap and is immediately afraid.

The two queens carry away the spectre made of cheese-cloth full of bad air.

The great insulin syringe drank my body into a bread-crumb of eyes all talking at once, then shook them dead.

I could still see a slender loris with lemonade eyes, an aviary of shadows, a baboon spider in bed with me. A wide blort mouth and silky whiskers.

A century of Shakespearean oaks comforts me.

I am standing at the altar. The cathedral begins to pitch and roll. Spray dashes against the great East Window. The organ blares a melodious warning and the great vessel struggles over the waves. Coloured scenes of the bible story shine from our windows over the approaching chalk-cliffs. There is a door opening on a vision of health after long illness.

A lighted staircase, and the small rose-hillocks of her breasts imply a flock of infant gazelles feeding.

The father leans against the heavy mantelshelf, most elegant in a shirt of deep frills. The shirt is very white, his hair very black.

There is a green square among houses. The child toddles over the warm carpet. Now the winter comes down over the square in flakes as heavy and soft as the deep frills of his father's shirt.

xv

Ecumenical

She is not in her dotage with her ecumenical medicines. She communes with the elixir of yeast: it contains three hundred essences of herbs the yeast has fed on and now lifts to her mouth. She drinks down the living yeast; she drinks down the clothing of the hillside. She swallows the gleaming tabsule of trace-elements from the rocks beneath the flowers of the hills she worships; the molybdenum and zinc beneath the marjoram and hops, ivy, rue, passionflower and elder.

Her pension dwindles and cannot afford the jelly of the queen bee convening all the flowers of the summer with the bee that travels into the heart of every flower on the hill.

The words 'Royal Jelly' bring the fizz of a few drops of clear colostrum to her nipples. She was accustomed to soak these drops up in dry biscuit and consume them again. Now she washes them off into pure water with a pledget of cotton wool, and sprinkles the flower in her window-box. The bees will take it.

XVI

Sometimes an egg, sometimes a shell, sometimes a snake
This morning I take my usual walk over the pasture. Edward, my collie, finds something unusual in the valley. He is barking like a regiment of musketry.

Here he comes over the rise dragging a darkness that looms over us like a mansion. It is coiled like a snail-shell, but large as a manor house made of brown fingernail.

I toil to the crest of the hill and look down into the water-meadows, which are strewn with other shells.

Now I use these coiled shucks as silos, brans and grain-bins. Their yolky contents weigh them down. They cannot blow away. Through the walls I can see the lamp in my wife's hand as she winds through them. The seed keeps well in the horny snail-light.

I believe they may be the successive distinct shadows of a spiral galaxy that passed in the night.

Sometimes an egg and a stone, sometimes a sea-shell, sometimes a snake.

A serpent darted out from behind the murdered girl's photograph. The brass tray rang out with the strike. Venom spotted nanny's apron. She loved the venom in the wires. Blue-white venom, with crackling scales. Once she had seen it naked leaping between the generators in the Science Museum, another time from cloud to cloud at the height of the storm.

The family's house was a conservatory of serpents, with room after room of them woven in the wall. She sat with her radio between stations, to catch the echo of the crackling tails.

She arranged flowers in circuit-patterns. She put out milk for the electricity. That section of the serial picture on the wallpaper, the brook behind the bookcase, was used for bathing. She heard splashing and wallowing as she lay in bed in the dark, glimpsed scudding mists of boiling.

She liked spots on her uniform. She daydreamed of a serpent in its death-throes, it laid its head the size of a cottage on the edge of the cliff and vomited into the green valley. A rain of torn fragments of goat and whole monkeys, mucus like coloured mackintoshes.

She stood in her clean nurse's uniform watching, then walked into the spray. The snake bellowed with a roar that shook round the mountains and its last resources of pearly venom squeezed from its jaws fell through the air in the shape of a Medusa, struck her, clung and spread, buzzing with toxicity, and her skin flushed and itched and she came.

Sam, Dorothy and the twins were her responsibility.

The dead as unhappy and happy as that, pleased with a plastic flower.

The other side of the tree is hollow and stamped with numbers.

Men moving the dolls through glass corridors in the kaolin dawn.

The wise glare. He weighs nothing, like the evacuation of light, as a lighted lift slips down a dark building. A bright light shines from her important place in the sealed cask.

But he made the return journey as relics, in a stone boat covered with toothmarks. This boat had been promised for a lintel-stone to bless the well.

The pond came like a glass udder walking on its teats down to the sea's edge for its blessing.

The faithful chaplain bit off a finger and ran with it carried in his mouth. To bless the people. She suckled the child through her warty witchnipple. To bless the people. The king's wizards lost their heads, pumping into the skyhead from seven faithful channels. To bless the people. She stole her father's serpent of wisdom, she had her breast out, it was smeared with goose-fat and soot. She sloughed off the old nipple, the golden button grew beneath. To bless the people. The wise baby drank from the golden tap and the air was full of the conversation of animals. The wizards heard this through their raw stumps, twice over. The serpent gave up its wisdom. The king heard little. The ants built their nests, to bless the people.

XVII

The molecular liturgy

From head to foot.

The birds that leave no stain upon the air.

Treading the spinal ladder, from head to foot.

He opened the door in the root, there were hurrying streets.

He closed it, he was naked.

He opened it and acquired a loincloth which was bees swarming when he closed it. He walked away on tiptoe, hearing through his groin the whetting of their stings.

The star walks over the earth and its footprints are beehives.

By profession, she is a lady of the rocks.

She knows the craft of the third eye sitting among caverns. The lid of ignorance sleds continually there, the inner sun beats its wings, the tiny tot dwarfed in the cerebral armchair inhales the wing-draught sleepily.

The boy in the boat is his sister below: a feathery touch rebounds to the skull's roof. Light pours through the black hair from the transparent skull.

The birds return, their flock forms into a crumpled mask as big as a sail over me, which nods, and sweeps away.

To see a ghost in the middle of the dance-floor? What else is a dance for, but for the raising of ghosts! Every pond a tall stare. Every penis a cool corridor.

The niceties of the situation give them a second look at the plums and peaches.

A skull rests on the beach, grinding its jaws.

Every cell of his flesh has a tiny grain of sand in it, which rattles as he walks. The accumulated sound is the swish of skirts, the swish of invisible skirts always around him.

In what week does he decide to become a man? In the Month of the Kraken, the Week of the Medusa.

All have gone on the journey. Some think the great toe was formed first. The grey woman breathes on his eyes and he goes blind. Her name, Worry.

I had these pure and virgin apprehensions from the womb. Dreams talk back to life in its own tongue.

Prenatal baptism by his dad. But this was the falling of the roof of the room under the waves, we joined together, we braced and tried to keep the snake from spitting, both of us, the room and I.

Now smash the plastic chariot of black knobs, white dials, the rigid rosary watchtower! Draw out the geranium entrails, discover the firm wrinkled jelly, rapidly cooling. Nerve-box sideshows. Shadow cave on the wrong side of time. Dreamgelder.

XVIII

Sun-stones singing

Swimming among the sun-microbes, the spirochaetes of sunshine, I catch love, badly. The church grows a beard. It is appletrees and lichen, full of birds and rain. Lichen altarcloth-transplants. Applewarehousechurch. Warehousemenpriests. Full fruitwharfage and waterwaftage.

In some applewarehousechurches the fruit grows dry, wrinkled and sweet, and the closecongregation of lawnworshippers munch them through winter.

In certain other holyapplestorehouses they rot in storage and make applebrownspirit. Naked celebrants leap into the nave with wooden spades. They smash out at the ciderdecay and it makes them drunk with spiritous bruising. They scour and hoe the building carrying out lumps taller than themselves moulded by groyne and gargoyle, vault and pillar, edible architecture joyfestering on the grass slopes.

Codling maggots fizzle and squeak in hot fat over bonfires like applefritters, or they are taken home and pampered like puppies with apples. They are kept in muslin cages until they turn into moths. Then they are shaken out into the sunshine to fly away and infect with inebriety other churches.

Alas

Possession by fiddler. His right of way my ear-parting. It is certainly not wronger than anybody can imagine. For nine other lives the chime went into the ear. And neither person could make the other happen. Delicious favours were forced. So were the pallid signatures that afforded no greater sum than the sum of all their miseries, which came like hot breaths off all their wire-coloured shirts. Always the husk, always the covering, always the doily. Fat, and no cigar. The favour of the quintessence rules upwards. The sky rests in the voile of seaweed. Oh what pleasure prevents me sight-mindedly. Fall-minds and the decisions of the makers. And they go. Slide-rules, adding the deficiencies. Try this keen famishing. Stroke the blunt puzzle. Cartridge a grief-claw gauntlet. The love-bear in the corridor. The hand-moving bracelet, unclipped, lets it fall. Oh Love, what splendid sweeps and blended saps your limbs seem in petition with the deed. The eyelid dead.

A tree throws down its library of books every autumn, it throws out all these books, and it grows new ones. A tree takes off its brain, throws it to the ground. It shatters. A new brain grows. First acid green, then olive and darker greens. In its fevers it racks stained stairways like a sunset. Insects delight in autumn before they depart for their sealed vials of ichor. The tree throws down acorns like ichor-flasks of forests.

Walking or skating on the flat leaves of the great tree, skating over the layer of hard wax of the bubbling cells, the stomata like ladies swathed in green furs, parting their tippets as the sun-shapes ride across, like living well-heads. It rains, one may scamper for shelter or stand to the bucketing drops of blue-tinged electric-tingling water. In this tree-bark are many mansions.

The feathers that travel. That have control over the wind. The whirlwind that travels on the moth's back. The desired girl could step on the design and be safe for life. But first his rock turns to fluff, and his armour to bird-down.

The swallows beating their wings in unison shape a pearly whirlwind, hoop or mirror that bounds over the stubble. There is a wooden skull with an acorn rattling in it. I hold it up. Fear and meat comes and goes over their faces. Seven witch-doctors attempt to supersede me, dowsing with lasers. One finds oil in me, another blood, the next appletrees and cider, the next ladies combing their long fair hair, the fifth pigs, the sixth a new leaven, and the seventh himself in a jar that was larger inside than it looked.

Nobody complains at that age, it is said to be an unlucky number. There are three uses of the head to be learnt. As a companion at feasts, for butting down doors and for kissing. Sums come from a ticking heart, mensuration is done with the bowels. The all-powerful maid servant told the little boy his bedtime stories and slept with him for her own pleasure, and he nearly thirteen, early for his degree. He has quite lost the habit of many things the body is good for besides going to the pictures. Past the other tower I can see the undulating meadow foothills, and among the clouds, the peaks of the mountain. The room in the other tower is ruined.

Cracked and broken windows and profusion of ivy pouring from them like an open tap. There are books there, manuscript and drawings, much faded. I preferred them to my own volumes that maintained themselves vividly, I was tired of that over-confidential and mechanical approach and spent much time poring over the whispered volumes.

At the mountain-top, an observatory. Beneath the lake, a submarine. On the left, the warm tower, and on the right the wind whistles through the broken stones.

The core of the whirlwind. The air is perfectly still and fresh. It smells faintly of ozone. The walls are smooth, and shine with great velocity. They reflect my image, which towers over me. I step closer and it acts like a shaving-mirror, showing me the pores of my skin.

The floor is membranous and invisible; rubbery but firm. Silence is perfect. The light is adequate, nervous and tinny.

I am carried at the height of a church steeple over a land I glimpse only. The switching maw of the wind allows me glimpses only. The lumpy brown ridges of a ploughed field that suddenly leaves its level and flies up towards me in fragments, parting before my invisible platform and melting into the mirror-stillness of the walls I dare not touch because of their velocity, which show gritty for a moment.

I pass over a farmhouse, which springs up towards me like a lover running. But a lover who loses the fingers of his hand as he runs but can't be bothered, then the arm, then his teeth and head in a soundless scream, and finally the legs get to me and have nothing to say. This house leaps upwards in a shower of towels and bedlinen, tiles and the broken treads of a staircase. I watch a sleeping face wreathed in bedlinen smile through the wall before the mirror-surface sucks it beneath. The head of a woman with feathered hat prods through with terrified eyes and disappears, before she can scream, into the reflection of my opening mouth.

If I tire of the silence I may walk into the wall with outstretched finger. The whorls and beads of sweat in my fingerprint will show for the instant before I am snatched by it and pulled, a crippled twist into the sky to fly like a husk or be laid in the water-meadows.

But now it is a split-second world of womb and nerves and rubbery glimpses.

xx

Then father comes
In the form of a God like a bull made of feathers. A semen-spout in the shape of a woman jets out of the top of his head.

The winds of the earth also jet, from the northern and southern hemispheres and collide with great turbulence at the equator; the two airshellhalves chafe sparkling sooty thunderstorms.

Every body of water has a natural resonance. Moses opened the Red Sea with his cries.

The last wave came with a hollow roar and a luminous

glow.

They brought out the great tears and laid them in the centre of the table.

He has an oblong sapphire he can detonate with a burning-glass, but only at midsummer. Then winter begins.

XXI

Notice Jesus

XYZ was hurrying from Rome when he met J travelling the opposite way. 'Why, J,' he said, 'what business have you in Rome?' 'I am going there to be crucified again,' replied J. XYZ was so ashamed he turned round and went back to Rome.

Now he is on the tree, upside-down.

His mouth is the great rooting breath. His lungs turn inside-out with each breath, ramify through the earth.

His anus is like a sailing-ship, on fire with electricity in a thunderstorm. Lightning flickers over a shit sea. The crowds are delighted.

The crowds are delighted, laughing and pointing. The crowd wears clean robes. XYZ is thoroughly dirty at both ends. His skin is inside-out and his thoughts crawl all over it. You can see his seams, throbbing.

XYZ is busy, for the tree has got him. I walk there a century or two later. The bark is a hundred or two hundred years thicker. An inverted crucifix? But XYZ has the keys.

The snake sits in his coils, and threatens us with whirl-winds.

A wind got into the millstone. We sat dead-heading the young whirlwinds. Two of them collide and fight, trampling the waters.

A tsunami appears, rushes on.

The green lady sits on a mossy gate swinging her lithe legs.

She is resting. The bucket of ball-oil is heavy. The windy staircase is high and slippery.

She enters the turret. The big lamp flickers, but she has

113

ball-oil, in a bucket.

The sufficient light beams out. The world begins again. She curls up on the floor watching that unfurl itself.

I jump and twist, falling squarely on my feet, and run! I have avoided a blow from the hoof of a hitherto invisible dinosaur.

I stand in front of the fall of water. My reflection faces me. It stands in a bolster of foam and spray. It weeps and gashes continually, its voice is a burr of thunder. The armoured men walk through it towards me. King Arthur, Charlemagne, Alexander, Freud and Jung. I stumble through the rocky pools towards Jung. He looks at me kindly. I reach up to kiss him but his bad breath makes me dizzy.

A mackintosh or a shadow flutters in the stream and when I bend to pick it up I find that it is a cave in the stream. I step in and pull it up over me.

I am in armour, facing a waterfall. Through the water I see sunshine and a girl standing on the bank, looking anxiously in. I stalk through the fall, the water thunders on my helmet, the girl rushes towards me and tries to kiss me, but faints into the stream. I tear off my armour and the darkness pours out. Much of it washes away on the stream. Some remains fluttering in the water like a rag of shadow. The girl revives and steps into me. A few glittering sand-grains from her shoes fall to the stream-bed.

He grips me hard. I am an ice-cube, I chap him and I melt through his fingers. He shouts at me and I am a tiger but I am frightened of his bullets and I melt like varied flames through the forest paths.

He shouts at me again and there is nothing for it but to be one of the ringing syllables that shock the ceiling.

Then he swears at me and I am a small turd that lurches out of my tail. With my finger to my mouth I try to make off but I trip over my leash. Then he shouts at me again and I am a lady ice-cube and a tigress and a vagina-syllable, and a ladylike turd scented with rosemary. I have learnt female, so now I will lock myself in the lavatory and grow a great hag of shit for him. I will crush her against my chest and let him worship those murdering breasts.

XXII

No psychiatry without penalty
The skulls left on the beach.

For the dead to pick up.

They watch the talk of the living through the dead shells.

A dead woman walks on to the empty beach.

She thinks, the living overcrowd that beach, there would be no room for me.

The dead woman picks up the shell, she can hear the live sea breathing from its tip.

She looks up. She observes her dead sea of dry ashes. She bends to the shell again.

She walks across her empty beach listening to the living at the tip of her shell.

There is a snatch of radio music from that transistor, the wail of a child complaining about the ice-cream, the petulant stutter of a lover who wants to leave the crowds.

She places the shell with invisible hands over my heart and listens to its beat.

Men ought not to wear knots in their clothes. Lying in this attic he unknots his clothes.   '

There is a long shell on the chest of drawers like a knotted thighbone. There is a skeleton wearing a dress of shells.

A shell understood is a knot untied. I cannot die because the door is bolted.

The sepia soul conceals itself temporarily among the hanging mackintoshes. The candle spills out its winding-sheet.

All things begin to untie themselves. Untied they are water. Water reties itself and becomes you.

Death is transparent, I watch the clockwork inside his case. I tried to unshuck the girl but she wouldn't come.

The wind stood on tiptoe and began treading out a pearl-dance over the oyster-bed.

Purity hides in the water, under the bearded and hag-fissured shells, is reborn through water and spiral. The serpent is a shucked seed that wings through the air.

Now the sun ploughs a spiral track across the world's air, winding all the clocks.

The earth-clocks are made of glass and metal, or sand and vibrating quartz-crystals in which a pure note is imprisoned.

There are clocks mensurated by tuning-forks, clocks that speak aloud the time in verse, clocks that deliver printed horoscopes (the stars are always watching, always working).

There are chiming clocks, and clocks that chime once only, on a quick fuse.

There are sun-dials, and clocks that run on oil, on tides and electricity, on the magnetic flux of the earth.

There is the pace-maker set into a man's diseased heart.

There is the gas-flame clock of Bunsen that vibrates to a musical note, and time passes quickly where there is music. There is the instant of a horoscope drawn at conception, and we remember that such is not mere diagrams and letters on a vellum, but fiery sparks in a blackness full of tinkling fingers.

There are wave, steam and droplet clocks, rain clocks.

There is the joss-stick clock that measures the Geisha's hours, the astronomical water clock of the Chinese that packs a mill-house.

There is the winter clock of chiming icicles, the potato clock full of sprouting tubers, the fir-cone clock that measures round its dial with cast pollen-shadows.

There is the clock that is a spinet full of mercury, and the clock that is a great blast-furnace, whose production divides the year into 100,000 ingots precisely, and whose flares and shadows are visible from the moon on the darkside of earth.

And the moon runs contrary to the sun pulling on the world's strings and sounding-plates of water, producing sounds which I cannot hear but which are clearly seen.

She is a maimed clock with a little blood at six o'clock, and she moans as the hour strikes.

Nail him to the estuary flood.

Close his body within a shell of blossom.

The tomb is a shell of flowers picked out in parables.

Now it is stone and lichen. He is now moving at the speed of stone, but speaking out of many books at the rate men read.

He breaks his slabs. His head like a green negro appears between the roots of the tree. He grins. His teeth are Greek letters.

Now he is serious. His eyes open and we fall into them, into a snowstorm of scriptures.

Because he will not speak to us but sends us letters instead, we believe ourselves to be at liberty.

He grins once more and his teeth are constellations that mark his food with horoscopes.

Now we are alone in the frosty night. I hurry over to my friend and speak to her. My warm breath makes white letters in the night air.

He played the harp but I heard no sound there was a succession of fragrances.

He took his crown he put it on my head and kissed me but there was still no sound.

And he took me by the hand and led me to the sheer cliff that falls from heaven to earth and I saw the wind come from the stars and move the clouds with no sound and I could read the scriptures the clouds spelt to all men in white letters but I could hear no sound.

And then the cliff split and there was a great winding staircase leading down of jasper and sardonyx that ended in the green plains of earth, but as the rock split and the angels lined my way throwing down scrolls before me on which were written the parables of heaven, I could hear no sound.

And I came down among men and the cliff sealed itself with turning strangely and with distance and men moved with me near and far but there was still no sound through that air and distance.

And men wept and spoke to me and I could not hear and I gave them my smile and put my hands on their heads and healed them and devils sprung out of their mouths like thrumming black twigs and wounds healed but they clapped to silently.

And I stood in a place where they had built me a very great church and the air behind me built up into a ladder to heaven, broad and spiral and the angels carried me back to him and he smiled without speaking.

Do not hurt the oil. He handed me a small bottle on which was written, Do not hurt the oil.

I took the oil on my palm and I spread it on my head. And then on my breasts, and I smoothed my hips over with the oil.

And a voice came from the oil. It said, Do not hurt me.

And a voice came from the skin I had oiled. It said, Do not hurt me.

And a voice came from my brain out of my mouth and it said, Do not hurt me for I am growing.

And I closed my eyes and I saw there in my head the oil that had the shape of my brain, and the currents began flowing in it downwards like two flanks of a running horse.

And all the currents chafed themselves into a downwards fountain and pushing out of it downwards a golden whiskered face which laughed and chattered upside down between my knees.

And I walked through the sand and my footprints arranged themselves into script which said, You cannot hurt me. And I walked into the streets and the same letters burned themselves like glass into the rock-pavements. The prince of the power of air now whispers to me like an ant as big as a horse, a mouse as big as a sow, a spider as big as a star and made of tin that creaks, an octopus as long as Henry, a bath-mat as big as an orchard, and the smells hanging on all the trees, a sun as small as a nut and very very hot, a desert as small as a soap-dish that drinks all the water.

Having done his first job he dips his paw into the sea and scoops out a jellyfish which he ties around his waist like a bustle with its trailing girdles and, notwithstanding the torrents of eggs that cascade from it backwards, flies up to heaven.

The seed of the Medusa floats for weeks in the air like thistledown and as it alights on flesh it flares, leaving a patterned burn like a snowflake. Some settle in the earth, and in crevices between buildings.

Which topple as it grows, the earth heaves, the cities fall, and the Medusa-seed grows a new city of windows and golden membranes in which the air is always fresh.

Next I worship an idol of wood. I carve inscriptions that fit together like bricks or like the marching footprints of a regiment. Then I install a high priestess and the heads tumble as she passes by.

four

The infestation of divinity

A small herb stares at me with clear brown eyes.

Mermaids tunnel in the river-banks.

I open the door to a stranger. His eyes are my own. She opens the door to me.

The garden earthworms have white beards, and are portions of a white-writing oracle. As I trowel the first hole, do what thou wilt: from the rosebush roots: shall be: from the thrush-carcass by the stone wall: the whole of the law.

The ghost of a plague of fleas whisks through the kitchen.

In the cellar are portions of a ghost becoming a god. The understairs is full of golden smoke and a single unconverted jaw-bone hanging in mid-air.

Women promenade muttering prayers and turn suddenly into what they will: a stone, a fountain, a pattern of trees.

It is time for tea. The sardine-tin is as big as the tea-tray and the key a crow-bar. The metal revers shows me the interior of a witch of many tails, her sinuous walk. I watch the tawny mirror carefully, and then we put each other back into our skins.

Her skirt was spinning so fast in a contrary direction I sprained a wrist getting it off.

What she said was so interesting I could not get out of the orchard, out of the supermarket, out of the London square, off the Cornish beaches.

The softness of her skin was grimpen of velvets, butter and primroses.

Interstellar space was no void of dead – immense, cold, without life. It was warm and full of symmetries, inclinings, rays and messages carried in the hands of bright pictures and memories. Her mother had been like iced sherbert strewn with rose-petals.

The snail cancels the difference between its end and its beginning.

It remembers itself completely, and there is a stud of pearl riveted to the leaf. The track of slime approaches, and ceases.

They made their churches in the garden out of the mist from the little stream. You could see the snails gliding out like cowled monks and taking up their appointed positions. By the stream was a small clearing with a ruined tree-trunk, powdery, moist and emblazoned with fungus. They gathered here, cobbling the ground and hanging in knotted masses from the hemlock stems. I thought they would return while the mists were still milky and the pavements wet. But at dry noon there were only these immense pearls on the half-eaten hemlocks and dockweed, and at the foot of the nettle-plants.

Sticky snailtaillights weave a great landscape. The path riveted with sunbolts, polished cracks and windows. Her lips taste the waves, the pebbled beach, the sun, before replying. She has acquired great strength and truth from this survey.

The tilt of her hatbrim tells me this, it is a little sample of the saltiness of the bay. Its shadow across her cheek states certain edges of sunshine. Nails: ten painted stones that can dance in parade.

I am trying hard to be nothing, but she loves me all the same. I know this in several ways, the line of her skirt shows me. My body in its yellow shirt and trousers of yellow, with its wristwatch and pocket of loose change, is a flapping page of her sunny seascripture.

There are shrouds moored to mountainpeaks. My fourth body plucks an apple for her from the tree with the watching roots. The stem parts with a twang like a bridge breaking. She shakes her head sadly and takes it from me, sinks her teeth into it with a sound like breaking waves.

Crab-claws and sharks-eggs a hundred feet long. Scoured out, a salty bungalow. Fishscale windowpanes. Soft white whalesgut vellum for carpets and bookbindings. Mesentery curtainflounces. I prop my fanged doorway open with a sea-bleached shipwreck. I sprinkle fine white sand for our bed. I light our lamp in the husk of a cray-fish. The ghost of the crab will bring its valved heart of five storeys for us to live in next summer. Light shines through these pleasing buildings; our bedlife of shadowplays.

The white prism rests upon the green book. It makes a light staircase downwards into the green book.

The pantlers of the ivy open their green cupboards crammed with veined fruitful musts. It is an excellent bramble, stacked with larders, hinged leaves arranged on stout spiral stairs. Its small thickset apples are chewed to bring madness. It begins with the initial 'I' which is the most human letter and as bright in colour as the new-born child.

It is the crab of the vine. Those grape-bladders are full of cloying, but in ivy the harsh wine is always mature. Its property is that it tears you to pieces if you do not speak when the time comes.

My bones waxed old through keeping my peace. This is a juice for fallen people. Damps linger all day on the staircases of the ivy. It is a wardrobe of white ghosts in cold weather. It is a rising staircase of doors stating a formula of great elegance and concision. Its greater name contains millions of numbers. Its winding about the world in strong lights creates eyes in the ghosts that peer between these doors.

The iceberg is a true ivy spiralled on these principles, but the leaves are of ice and close-packed, and the ghosts trapped. Ghosts should be free!

The fire in the iceberg. I stand there as the church melts releasing stored sounds, services chanted, organ anthems, ringing bells, all that has soaked into the ice stones now becoming music water. Only an empty space is left, tolling high in the sky. A hand reaches out of the space, feels about, tugs it larger. A sky-face leans in, smiles, disappears, the hand comes back and hangs a bell in the air. Then the bell begins to ring and from its mouth a pile of stones drops with clatter and dust. Now the chimes shake sense into the brick, shiver out staircases and pinnacles, pews and galleries, it tolls out a long nave with segments and with sharp tones clears large windowspaces for the sun to shine through and read the walls inside.

The new stone hewn out by the bells is bright and the colour of beach sound, the woman is a priest and dressed in white lace warbled out by the small bells. The service of warm rain begins falling as she speaks, gathers to torrents as the organ plays and the choir sings. The bright water unites our skins. The rain grows plush velvet moss over the pews and flowers the moss, our skins smell the clean chalky moss presence. Our wet clothes gently clasp our genitals, our nipples show through, our wet hair grips us and we struggle naked out of the cumbering to embrace.

The dawn is a time of great danger.

A cough sounds like a shot.

I am clasping a hand out of the cloud.

The open wings of the beast are settling, and the tree looks small.

The air is full of bird-shadow like wisps of black smoke.

There are no birds, the beast has frightened them away.

The beast settles on the grass and as it settles it dwindles.

Smaller and smaller, to a black stone, to a grain of black mustard in the grass-roots.

An ant comes stepladdering, kneels, picks up the grain in black secateurs, which close, crushing the husk.

The quick oozes white, a single golden drop follows and falls into the ground. The soil soaks it up.

A green tendril is snaking upwards.

In the house there are people watching the child in the grey uniform which is glacial black in the thunderburst.

He crouches himself like a closed knife, then the blade springs out! and the vine, tall and green, paunched with grapes, harbours a college of tiny talking snakes that are green.

The rooms of the house are full of panting ectoplasm which is gradually dissolving in the clean sunlight.

A hairy coconut with a kernel of crystal. The kernel crackling with light and cradled with down. I smash down the hammer. The globe is full of wax loops and petrified lightning. I strike again. It is pocked silver. I toss it in the air. It spins higher than I expected, clouds flood over it, it shines clear again with a pang, and I am crouched on black mud in the moonlight.

The mud is soft as down. I lay my cheek against it. And cold. I hear singing and I struggle to my feet, ankle-deep in gloss.

A man is leading a crowd of young men and children along the bank, they all have his face. They each have a patch of mud on their cheeks, high, on the bone.

I fling myself full-length on the mud. Mud appears on their clothes. I run under the waterfall. Their clothes are wet and clean.

I heat a circle of mud with a blowlamp until it is dry, until it is glowing, and the sun rises.

It's time to look for her downstairs. I step on the first dusty tread as I would into soft slippers. There is a thicket of sloughed mackintoshes hanging on the door. I descend with an oil-lamp through strenuous cobwebs, like walking through touch-paper into a firework. There is a smell of parched elastic and insects interested in their own symmetries, of wellingtons and ankle-deep mud. The flat will do nicely. Our wings will come here and perch, and settle into masks.

During a funeral I do not believe in bringing anything alive into the house, into the odour of cut glass, the smell of the luminous edge and the millinery of vengeance. The vases and the curtains are dead; the curtains fall in stone folds against the idea of day, the vases hold their roses alive far too long a time.

A flock of grace rubbing its silvery wings together.

A spongy carpet of frogs.

The panthers of the ivy padding among its sculptured lanterns.

The landscape in the skin, wear it or walk in it, at pleasure.

I do not proselytise for fire, unless it flows and pours like water.

I wear earth, its fine cotton spun out of it, grown in sunlight and air.

Innumerable lanterns fit together within the ocean.

The sea, with fists pummelling in it, the great shipwrecked cry of the burst boiler-room.

The bones of the hand caught on a ledge. Caught on a stone coping as if the rest of the skeleton had tumbled down the well, the hand-clutch could not stop it.

I brought them into the house. I jumped them into a box. In the morning, they had been laid out correctly, as for articulation, on the dresser. Swept into a drawer, they are reassembled on the dresser overnight. There is nothing supernatural about the instruments of reassembly; a family of voles handles it. The voles are possessed.

I left them undisturbed on the dresser. Next morning, dry leaves were wrapped like cigar-leaf around each bone, for skin. Under this, gossamer and dandelion-seed for flesh. Grass-stalks for veins. A bracelet of blood-red berries at the cut wrist. Bits of snail-shell closely nibbled for fingernails.

It is the hand of an old woman. But the next morning, it has grown smaller, a child's hand. Cherry-petals for the skin, and under, firm appleflesh round the bones. The day is too long, the petals have begun to freckle at nightfall, and the browning of the apple shows through.

The next morning it is gone.

Sarah: small mole on chin, wide mouth, thin lipstick. Attentively-cocked head, unusual in elderly woman. Bones: chalky.

Silas: broad-banded Mexican tiger-moustache. Hands deeply freckled down to the bones, which are seamed and stained with tobacco-colour.

Teresa of the miracles: black, fey and witty. The miracles of her nickname are not virginal. Sometimes glittering and soft in manner: then Silas says she is like a jelly blackcurrant fruit pastille, sprinkled with glittering teeth. It is her party manner. Her body is an apparatus of black porcelain vases from which she pours and gathers herself up continually. Silas thought her bones must be painted in barbaric colours, tribal, ochre and crocus-powder, gold-leaf, down to the smallest knuckle-bone, or tiny shell deep in the ear. It is untrue. They are white and plain like anybody else's.

Jonas: tall and too blond. Bones like glass, full of cold and stony dreams.

Tomas: scribbled in chalk. Accident-prone. Handbones like bitten lead pencils. The skeleton is surprisingly small. Our memories of him are much larger.

Jesus: has more bones than anybody, some of which are still in use, others scattered on far shores.

Sandy: no bones, no trace. Look in the fire for me, was his last remark. Could be an avatar of Jesus.

Scrimshaw. Scrimshaw.

five

Wet dream, wet girl

Walking across dark water on silver crutches. Riding across dark water with a silver sundial as a raft. He was tied to the upright post. He struggled, and as the right hand strap broke, he woke.

Silas believed in eating the dream. He enacted it awake. Metal would not carry him across water. It would have to be wood, silver-painted. Or a raft of willow-logs, naturally silver. The upright gnomon plaited from osiers.

He could not observe and float. Teresa would have to crew, on the flooded water-meadows. She would be lightly-bound with withies.

She turned up in a long dress. This at first he thought unsuitable, but her remote beauty in it persuaded him. He bound her, he launched the raft, and a small breeze sprung up, spreading choppy wavelets. Teresa declared the raft to be unsafe: she wanted her arms in case she had to swim for it. She struggled with her bonds and slipped one hand free, but the raft swung and slapped the surface sending up a cascade of water. The wavelets suddenly looked like the teeth of clockwork, and Teresa stood there, drenched and laughing.

He took her home in her long soaked dress and drenched hair, gave her a bath and towelled her dry, and they went to bed. Silas' dreams were full of water and grass, and Teresa walked across the water to him without the aid of the crutch he had invented for himself.

Machines that were machines in so far as they had moving-parts, but which made nothing useful, fascinated Silas. Clocks particularly, which were for chopping nothing into equal portions, irritated him. He wanted to make growth-clocks that operated without noise and suited a world of floating days better than the fiscal guillotine movement that was always trying to scratch its way back through the mirror.

They lived together in the seed of the flower, in the oak's acorn.

As soon as they moved into the cottage, he fitted up an outhouse as a workshop, with lathes, watchmaker's equipment, and micro-welding apparatus.

The hair of the cadavers in the medical school turned sandy in the pickling tanks. Their eyes were white and blind under the eggshell eyelids.

In his workshop Silas apprenticed himself to the construction of measuring instruments, micrometers.

Tomas visited the cottage, he wanted to buy the land. It was empty and derelict, with bitten walls and weed-stuffed gaps. The boys from the village school said it was haunted by a sandy-haired old man. They used to go out of their way home to break the windows. One little boy remembered throwing a rock at the big french-window. As it left his hand he saw, he said, the lean figure of the sandy-haired man nodding and smiling at him from the glass in the instant before it fell, shattered into many woodland reflections. Tomas could feel Silas and Teresa living there, though he saw nothing. He found in the chimney-nook one of Teresa's barbarically-painted pots, burst with a shower of roots by the briony that was growing in it. Back through the press of shrubs and stems the briony deep-coiled into the woods. The broken chimney stood sheathed in ivy. He thought he saw Teresa's shadow in the lane, a shadow with flowing hair. The clouds above seemed like her shadow, white, with flowing hair. He and Sarah wanted to get married. She was a very good listener. He decided against the site of Silas' cottage, and then felt ashamed.

Silas made a tiny planetarium in his workshop. It incorporated a miniature welding shop, a forge and a glassblower's bench automated by micro-miniaturisation and a computer.

Turret heads carried astronomical telescopes: it made models of the night, in platinum wire and glass. You selected the correct telescope, and left the assemblage out overnight. In the morning you opened its doors and pulled out a perfect representation of the telescope's visions; traced out like wire sculpture on the glass axis of the pole star. You could also observe a trypanosome under the microscope, and the same apparatus would construct a model of it, beautifully welded and coloured. Or the tracks of twenty-four hours in the life of a human phagocyte, or the operations of a tissue-culture, obsessed with rebuilding its animal out of itself.

Silas and Teresa loved machines whose products were ruminative and not utilitarian. They fed microphysical equations into their 'planetarium' and an hour later received the equivalent object. They learnt to feed those three-dimensional star-maps back into the apparatus. In time they received first plants, and then living animals walked out of the doors. Then they dispensed with machinery. Teresa breath-fired a ceramic decorated with sigils of the briony. Silas spoke a thrush out of clay. It staggered out of the mud with every feather perfectly conceived, stabbed around in the grass for a worm, flew away out of sight. Teresa entered a sculptor and they learnt to guard their days together with clocks that were masses of terracota and unfissured stone, but she was not away from Silas for an instant.

I heard of the cottage in the oak wood from Tomas. I decided to sleep for some nights in the ruined building. I was aware that the dead, pressing on the living slantwise, pressing upwards from the grains of soil, from the atom itself, created strange living forms in the receptive but fallen brain. Animal and plant life grows from them perfect in its symmetries, but the human living are fallen, and their dreams *press* upon them from their perfect flesh, where the dead have their factories. I believed that there were only two dead people. One was black, and a woman, and one was white, a man-child. I was prepared to relive horrors of the death-trauma, and the ecstasies of life re-making. These notes owe their origin to my sojourn in the ruined house. I am no one remarkable. I have sandy hair. In sunlight it shines like old gold.

Is this a gibbet?

There is a small body hanging from a stalk.

No black shadow of putrescence cast.

A roasting smell.

It is a ready-cooked piglet, warm and brilliant with grease.

And I see this woman tearing handfuls off the gibbet as I come to the tree again.

The liquid goodness ran down her chin on to her dress.

She turned and smiled and held out a handful.

The reek out of her mouth struck me in the face.

I fainted and woke up again under the oak-tree, near the drinking-fountain.

I hated the weather-lady, with one eye on the sky and the other watching the soil and her dark dress rent with lightning flashes, until I met the gibbet-lady.

Before this, the oak-lady had watched me out of acorns in a fissured face.

I come again and again to the tree and today a white rain lady makes mud at its foot.

Velleity paint, vertigo paint, altitudes printed over her dresses.

Opening of the staircase at the neck, big buttons of bird-skulls.

Leather dresses known to be chimp-skin, her wonder-awakening dresses, star-rays combed into a shaggy dress, bone-flounce skirt, turbinal blouse.

One dress that shimmers without slit or seam like the wall of an aquarium and a starfish moves slowly on its pumps across her bosom, passes out of view, a shark glides, a turtle rows silently between her knees.

And the dress of louse-skin.

And another of bird-cries and meteor-noise and declarations of love.

A dress of purple jam packed with tiny oval seeds.

130

Another of flexible swirling clockwork running against time.

Another of grave-soil that rends and seals as she turns.

And another of bloody smoke and bullet-torn bandages.

Ticker-tape.

Fishskin without slit or seam.

A glass bead.

A pearl.

An atom.

Mulatto children play among the bones.

Bones are toys for children who are toys for bones.

The vole family has custody of Teresa's thin white hand.

At the root of the apple-tree, Silas gives flesh to the fruit.

Teresa in the morning cloud; every evening she can be found below the southern terrace.

Sarah is almost geology and Tomas sits in a beach-stone.

Jonas is whale-seed, or sea-star glitter, does it signify?

The world is hung with bones and with fruit.

The bird cries out, and tosses its velvet antlers.

Trees understand language. Flourish! you say and it is thick with summer. Nourish! and it drops fruits.

Dreams strike upwards with the lightning into the sealed stone, and into the sealed head.

His fingernails on her white blouse looked like a row of red cherries, the great antlers of wine shone like the red hot mouth of the polar bear in the arctic cold.

Then I felt a pink spider-pain in my mouth, and I thought it was from never-melting mother into milk, and my eyes focused a nipple like a branching antler, and the red wine filled my empty cup and I poured it away and it filled again, a river of wine poured from that cup till it poured milk, until I had undrunk all that I had kept to myself, until it poured blood and sticky birth-water. Then she had for one instant a house of light.

A tall old man with green cowl and white hair glided behind her like a windflecked wave along the woodland path.

There were eggs of deep blue stippled with gold and a

worm-eaten wardrobe stuffed with dry leaves, and whispering low, and a little white spider of foam dancing on the weir-step.

And I felt the nail driven, as with a ceremony, driven in with steady blows.

The hoar rock sinks in a litter of twigs and leaves.

Blue hailstones.

Electric blue spume on the waves crackling with sparks, each bubble of foam encloses a tiny bolt of lightning.

His throat turns to gold as the brandy touches it.

A leafy corridor with lank cool shadows between rows of modern flats.

A fruitseller's barrow piled with sleepy pears, punky bananas, a chariot for the sleeper.

She has a telephone on her desk black as an unpaired shoe, the telephone she is crying into melts, she snarls with teeth black as telephones.

The wastepaper basket was full of greasy yellow bones.

In the evening she conducts the glass orchestra with a flashing transparent wand, it was a beach of foaming rock-spawn, greasy and glistening, sun and electricity.

A faint stirring and rattling as I passed by the shelves and millions of voices crying, feed me, feed me.

The pages clattered like oyster shells as I tried to read, she laid a finger on my shoulder and said, kiss me instead, and so I did, the pages clearing and opening like windows to fresh air. And I could still hear the voices ordering and cajoling from the telephone nerves of her teeth.

What are you doing, locking up the bed?

The cathedral is a chariot of stone that has parked and turned into a mountain. Once, before it was a stone, it was the bed of a holy man, from which he stared at the ceiling.

What's the perfume, I asked, smelling her. The murder of the egg, she replied in French. She wore a shimmering gown of cloth-of-bullet-lead. Her teeth sliced the knot-bread.

She throws her wedding dress into the fire – the ghost is alight!

I am clumsy, I am Leviathan, I am a whole nation, but the head at the crown of it all demurs and drops the mirror.

The king squats on my neck, I knot my tie around his lords, his smiths toil in my lap, his soldiers drop the glass.

I drive the big nail into the grave, deeply, I listen at its head, I jam it into the grate where the fire burns, I turn its glowing point in the air and listen to the horizon, I drive it in the shingle and listen to the waves, I wait for the thunderstorm.

I took the skull and I piled burning coals in it for a brazier, I packed it with mud and modelled convolutions, I rinsed it and dried it out and listened to the echoes. Then I filled it with seawater and watched the sun play in it. Presences came, I could not see them in the awake day, my dreams provided a carriage for them, a kiosk, a glass of brandy, a liqueur chocolate, a cinema ticket, a thundcry landscape. I saw the footprints of the invisible in the soft snow, in the tough bubble that walked in the rainstorm.

A gradient has been formed. The white veal cuts easily with a fork, milkily. I leave by the office window, I cling to the telephone wire. I tread the narrow edge with a companion who makes me frightened by screaming at the traffic sixty floors below. Then we turn the corner of the building and step down into a mossy clearing with a ruined chimney among oaks. A spring bubbles, the turf is soft. I embrace my companion in gratitude. The water in the spring changes to silk.

The great gorged cave of canes, the plantation of the organ, the congregation finds the music transposed over its skin beneath the clumsy Sunday clothes, serge and hats, they float naked in their clothes through the little Close.

And a hare starts up at her footsteps and a toad squats in his.

Now the organist joins them in his squeaky boots and all gather round behind him to find what the miraculous footsteps provide in his case. Doubloons? Meals for the needy? A magical horse, in sections? Nothing. Only a waver of tiny voices winding upwards. We all bend to a footprint to listen.

The footsteps whisper: I promise to be a better organist. I will be a better musician.

An initiate is one who can act as a spiral, but I am as puzzled by the sea as I am by churches. The sea, walking arm in arm with the great Jesus. A corduroy violin, a barley-sugar trombone. I can see my scream ebbing away among the flowers and sinking into the rocks. I didn't want to scream again, it covers her with wrinkles.

For the wife's white cheese frightens me, pungent and crumbly, her flanks warm and slippery, her eyes like black quicksilver, like moray eels, her plates of shell and bone, she lays me split-open meat resting on bone-china, cannibal feast. This one's wife will not have him. He lives in lightning, sulphur and ice. That one's wife prefers him with a smooth skin, and is surprised by an occasional wolf-grace in him. He would like to fly, on tiptoe. He raises his hands, they are webbed with blood. The flower that curses him is white.

White excitement grinning black lechery like a row of greasy telephones.

White clothes are a glorious joke: the sick folk are dying of laughter at the doctor's smock.

Brightly-clothed butterflies flutter over the quagmire.

The young alligator sings out that all writing is purple to him, and that no man he ate had any brains in his skull that he noticed. He crunched: nothing but a pocket of sweet smells.

What *is* behind the jokes, gentlemen?

The letter blew a jabbering fart as I ripped the seal.

The red swollen tie glints from his cut throat, the sweet-smelling oil lances into his trousers as the monster of Frankenstein staggers across the ballroom, the dancers screaming and scattering. The second under-maidservant advances without fear with her skirt lifted. The ointment pumps where it is received. The gigantic magistrate nods his head with a ringing of gongs. Hundreds of loose windows rattle like loose change at each detonation. Caterpillars pasturing in the great green sheds rear their whelked tufted faces. The haematite saints fall against each other with a clatter.

The little maidservant's neat uniform is covered with blood and dead twigs, her little twat is packed tight as an ointment box. Now she disentangles him because she wants to wash and bandage his poor neck. The touch of her ointment will soothe the neck, but the wound will not heal. Its edges will rest together, the love-mouth in his throat, and she will silence it sweetly with her long tongue.

He threw the knife into the field, over his shoulder.

A fresh knife grew in its sheath.

He wrenched the trouser-bottom from its short hawser.

Another budded from the snapped threads.

He flung the greasy black custard at the fresh linen smock.

The laundry man drove up with replacements.

He smashed the lighted oil-lamp on the wooden floor among the bales of millinery.

The director yelled 'Cut!'

He said his prayers leaving out the word 'God'; he cut all the angels' pictures out of his bible.

His head filled with a beating of wings.

He plucked slugs from the garden and saved them for her salad.

She licked her long lips.

He stove in the hull-boards of his children's dinghy.

Daddy! they cried, running across the river towards him.

He broke open a firework and sprinkled the grains over a trifle.

They solved the mystery of the universe over coffee.

He melted down his wife's suppositories and stuck needles into little models of her lover.

The daddy died, and she came back to him.

Dying back into my bath, thinking of my goat-trousered legs . . .

There is a sacred chancel at both ends, a rising and a setting at both ends, two sealed vases. Chessmen.

The policeman's conscience is kept behind the star on his helmet.

A chessman.

There is a little bench running around the inside of the altar-stone for debating ghosts.

All chessmen.

The little man carried a book that kept him invisible even while he was being decapitated.

A chessman.

He spent a long while gazing into the forest as if it were a library of pages infested with real teeth.

The forest is a chess-piece.

On the page-blade a slice of bleeding meat.

Paper takes meat.

Tennis-courts and goldfish ponds full of moonlight. I walk hand in hand with the mudlady.

She is a black queen.

The battlements of the manor-house are formed into letters that say 'My Father's Golden Book'.

My Father's Golden Book is a chess-instruction manual.

My father kneels weeping in front of the holy statue.

It is a chess-man.

Mescalin for the sun, cannabis for the moon.

Goodwill, vision, and honest blood spilt on the grey stone in strong sunlight.

Acceptance, abandon, display, and a long winding boatride under dark willows and a tubular sky.

The negro girl washed me carefully.

The goat-legged boy played a flute.

It chimed into me through the water.

The girl soaped my balls. She helped me out and we fucked among the tumble of warm white towels.

The goat-boy played on. His music filled the air.

These are my two friends who will never leave me, not even in the hanging dreams, the rough rope round my neck, my tears oozing sperm.

The clothes that tug around them work the guide-lines.

Seams and forks, all coloured! The white blouse works in colours, criss cross criss cross live dead live dead.

The triangle open at his neck points like a finger-post towards his pointing penis. Her shoulder-blades spar softly in her blouse, stretched radiations.

Wet clothes in the thunderstorm, the body materialised in the webwork of forces, under the trailing ectoplasm the dark smile of the breast looms forward through wet cloth, water tunes in on the nipple.

Wine gives colour and rapture that circulates in the cloth and spirals the flesh like vines. The shirt rips open with a disastrous newsflash, the flesh tingles in the sudden operations of the chrysalis . . .

. . . one of the echoes of the great tower and the iron bell of Babel wrinkling and writing over us so long not understood. Our clothes shall wrinkle and age for us. Two old ladies hobble uphill in their clothescrutches, their dresses bleed on the hangers all night in the sealed wardrobe, the flayed-beautiful young ladies embrace asleep.

A gale howls from the cathedral bell as it swings. He falls to clinker as the sound roughens his skin. He is a column of water emeried with chimes, ice crackles through him, he is a cloud of white notes that glitter as they explode. He is a flask of lightning, it bursts with thunderous peals, he has disappeared into one of the chiming atoms of the bell, he is the rim dwindling and roaring in pulses. The last note is a cool deluge expiring in waterweed.

I applied for the job and they wrote back to me immediately. I was to go for interview to a small northern town. The taxi took me to a school in the holidays, the school had battlements and large uncurtained windows. I was ushered upstairs through the chalky rooms. I was told to tune the bells. I had seen no signs of a belfry; I expected to find a sheaf of them jawing expected hours to all citizens from a tower high above the streets, full of punctual resentments.

But when I accepted the job they led me out of the school and through the town to the fields outside it and into the hills to an iron casemate-door set deep in a valley. They threw the door open and I saw the bells I had to tune hanging like a black thicket deep in the hill.

Their names were Bog Dog, Shivering Lady, Sonorous Earth, Treble Stone, Whanging Jill, Fairy Jug, Big Bottom and Dovetail Crime Robert. I had my brazier and my tuning forks and I brought the run to tune in a week.

Put your ear to the earth in the night when the city has stopped and you can hear them. They shiver the small wavelet-glitter in across the bay. They shake the small buds open. They age people and buildings with cracks. The baby and the mother hear them and cry out with the labour. They dry the pollen that vibrates from the catkins. The boulder bounds down the mountain-side and crushes the cattle byre. The mineral veins that stab through the earth to its core have picked up the tune and my forks buzz so hard that they scorch my fingers. They shake out three shadows from each man, woman and child.

It is painful for shadows to become white with no thickness like onionskins. They blanch with consideration. The black shadows that have not yet learned to become white crowd around the man with his head in his hands.

They are romantic. They came because they thought he was sorrowing about three trees that stand by his pathways, thickening with time-bark; his mother, his dead sister, his first girl. They are romantics, these shadows and they wish to learn blanching with consideration. The man however is picking his nose.

They stand astonished for a little while. They are romantics.

Then they begin picking their noses.

In no time at all they are standing on an impalpable rubble of shadow-snot. They are white to the bridges of their noses.

Then they are white to their waists.

At this point they have to ask a companion to help them. He rolls up his sleeve. He reaches in as far as he can. He is reached in.

The last scrape at the ends of the toes is difficult. They have to be shaken inside-out at the mouth.

138

Eventually all the shadows are white, like summer clouds.

They have learnt to blanch.

And what fun it will be to fill themselves up with dirt again, to shovel it up.

Already a filmy soot has gathered like a smudge on the gossiping profiles.

As for the man, he wipes his finger on his handkerchief, sighs, and gets up from the table where he has been sitting. He is only a man.

The shadows meanwhile are shrieking shadow, shovelling dirt into each other, then they will squat down and pick it all out together, and again, and again. But he is only a man.

On our way we saw a cyclist pedalling a small black thundercloud that flashed on and off. My father rowed out in the middle of the lake to the small bare island. He picked up one wet oar and launched it into the air like a javelin. It sped over the island humming, then suddenly checked itself by throwing out a shower of tendrils heavy with buds, starting a beautiful beech hedgerow that divided the island.

Then he threw the other oar, but this one went on across the island skimming the lake, and a white crack broke along its back, and a pair of wings like netted brocade flew from the crack, and its smooth length grew scales and a whelked and spectacled head until a giant dragonfly was rowing the air and disappeared into the trees on the opposite bank.

I took out my hip-flask and laid it on the top of a tree-stump. It turned into a yellow leather-and-glass beetle that struggled round the trunk's rim laying eggs like six sealed capsules. I popped one into my mouth and broke it with my tongue. It was full of brandy and a small meaty beetle-embryo, like a raisin.

Now I threw my black woollen cap in the air and it let out a thread which caught on a branch and there was a sooty spider with diamond eyes that began to shuttle out a web of furry wool.

Now that I had lost my black cap in the wood, I could see

everyone's brains like phosphorescent jellyfish with long trailing tails hanging behind their eyes, and the hearts like shell-less snails caught in the tendrils, whose eyes on horns stretched up to the skull-holes. These two creatures rested on a third like a ravishing bouquet of flowers at the pelvis, tied into a neat knot or bow at the genitals. This bouquet gave off a delicious perfume.

My father and I got into our thundercloud, switched on the lightning and moved off. It was time for tea.

The water is cool, and full of startled indignant faces eating earth. I step gingerly in among them.

This water is greasy with electricity. I swim, and my hair sparkles.

I get out. The splashes and ripples I make do not break the faces up like reflections, but simply loosen them, so they stream away on the current. Replacements arrive from upstream, and settle in the space I have made for them. Electricity from the current covers my body like silver fur, branches like lightning round my mouth and nostrils as I bend to kiss the black girl on the river bank.

Dance is the organisation of virtual powers. Here we have the thoughtful dancers, those whose task it is to suggest universities over the empty stage, mournful spectacles and encyclopaedias and always-falling fretful dust.

We have the pantomime illustrators, those who can fill a stage with heaps of broken custard pies through which they struggle smothered for a fresh shot. They are allowed no more than two wooden discs painted yellow for props.

We have specialists in the duck walk, a single squatting step. An hour long recital of three of these steps teaches more than the pantomime.

We have iconoclastic dancers, who first suggest vast and delicate machines, then dance their utter breakdown. Their hope is by imitative magic to extinguish the present age.

We have highly qualified teachers in a single subject, say stretching, or balloon-bouncing. There are courses in coital improvisation without partner, very ascetic and not popular with many students.

We are going along to the theatre now to watch the blind dancer, who puts aside his white stick as he dances, and creates for others visions of shape and colour that are unsurpassed, until he collapses in ecstasy and we send for his guide-dog.

These students in the wings are practising the basic bit-and-brace position together; fitted together in large partly architectural assemblages, they demonstrate the world's fabric of erotic forces on a small scale, say in a blouse-back, or a window-box.

I try to make him see what he has done. To take the sacrament through all the nine apertures! Sneering, he removed the swamp from his nostril. Half angry, he took the swamp with his tweezers and laid it on a sheet of fresh white paper. Half-sneering and half-laughing he plunged his clean shirt-sleeved arm up to the shoulder in the swamp. Withdrawing it, he examined the black satiny effect with delight. I could not restrain him.

Half inquisitive, half hysterical, he visited the swamp in his elbow. Then in his other elbow, in his knuckles in turn, while I waited by his empty chair. He returned as eels. Then he left and returned as toads. Then he left and returned as a lump of lead ore. He left and returned as a foul-breathed vulture which left.

Then he walked out of the vulture's droppings as out of a long white corridor with ragged black doors. He left clean-shaven, now he had a sandy beard and a long white burnous, like a bible illustration. I knew he would begin to quote scripture, so I opened the bible and left through it.

Arriving on Alpha Centauri III, a swamp came up to me and asked for an escort through the bible, offering me a pair of tweezers to handle the book with. I took the bible out of my pocket and pulled it up around us. When I came out of the white storm of swirling black particles, I was stuffing flour-paste as hard as I could into mouth, nostrils, eyes, ears, cunt and anus. I looked like a victim of a custard pie battle.

The priest held the oven door open for me. Ladies first, he said, as he turned on the gas and consecrated me. I lay back in the flames, said the bread, and resigned myself to beginning the journey again through the gates of the teeth, into the soil and the wheat-grain.

A grenade under a pie-cover dismantles the elaborate caisson of jellies in a split second, sticky festoons part slowly under their own weight, the ornamental custards are slags of milk-skin in loaded cobwebs.

The lightning strikes the water, delves and energises a deep ozonous whirlpool which condenses into an electrical plasma like a starfish that oars off with its spines bristling in rows like a fighting quinquireme, and a transparent carbuncle shaped like a woman with visible stone guts.

The latter falls three miles into the Challenger trench, down into globigerina ooze, to be recovered in rock strata three hundred million years hence.

The starfish rows out of sight, crackling with energy like a musketry range, leaving pungent blue smoke in puffs that condense into young jellyfish with trusting eyes.

The lightning strikes for a second attempt. The whirlpool rears itself out of the water with a shriek, the shriek becomes a scream rising beyond the limits of audibility. It lies sideways, and its speed is so great the hull floats on the water like steel. The inside walls bud off whirlwind ships officers, very tall and trim, with blue power shining at the eyes. They go about their tasks silently and efficiently.

The ship now tunnels beneath the earth to the radio station that is the magnetic core spinning like a dynamo, to augment the message broadcast through the millennia that screams out 'I have succeeded,' whispers, 'I no longer exist.'

A shattered glass self-echoed.

The deep entrance of the blind man's eyes.

The living man carrying the corpse-eyes in his sandy head, like bloodshot grails.

There's hope for ghosts despite the sunshine when the blind man goes tapping down the street.

142

There are many gaily-dressed holidaymakers with big eyes like mirrors hanging in front of whitewashed walls.

The darkness of the blind man's spectacles is piercing.

The walking imagination of darkness is abroad in the sunshine. Holidaymakers cast pink shadows with pale ties; his shadow is like a slot in the pavement.

Blazers become brighter, dresses more and more washable. The blind man could turn and walk back into his shadow, but his compassion rears his dark head in the street.

Any words he says have nightside meanings. No blind man could be eloquent: it would destroy us.

I ate an apple and my mood changed as the fruit shot its branches through me, branching apple-juice full of chattering birds.

Shifting the emphasis, I ate some porridge for the slow syllable of the oatmeal.

Now I took some chestnuts, for their brown monkey-skins.

This mixture alerted my shoulder-blades and nipples, and gave me a further triangle with its base upwards and following my collar-bone, the apex reaching down to the ligaments binding the two halves of my pubis. These to my great delight began loosening, so I looked about and into the cupboards for another food to encourage the process.

Rice? No, vinegar. I mixed a small quantity with water and drank it. This outlined my oesophagus and the roof of my stomach in a blue light recalling the shine of tin.

I needed greater pungency.

I sniffed the undiluted vinegar and a bright flap opened high in my nose which flickered lightning over a landscape below and slightly sideways, but the flap quickly closed.

The pepper-mill!

I snuffed up a quantity of the freshly-ground fruit and in bursts of sneezing from my solar plexus saw in a fresh light the thriving cities deep down in me that sent up also from arcing searchlights a pyramidal beam that showed us my head far above caught in the light laughing and sneezing.

Also there was the knife, the meaty ash in the drizzling

fire, the wallpaper thin as a shell. The orchard, far back and high in her body. She moves as the trees in her move.

But here and now we cannot feel or see the trees, with this greasy knife on the plate, the crumbs and the half-eaten cake.

I watch the cruet: a Woolworth's article in mock Jacobean moulded glass.

There! just for an instant in the split-second world the grains are precious, held gently in a formal system of windows, each one stating its presence of salinity or packet of ragged pungence.

Then my gaze skids on to the seersucker tablecloth. Strange, she is in seersucker too. My skin itches – then clears into windows among the rhythmic eyesparks and drizzling parklands of that folding fire.

The orchard in my girl, the towers of treasure, the window on prehistory, I am the dinosaur of mysticism and I wish I had been born a girl, dangerous and brilliant as gorse, or a brambled orchard of seasons and obsessions.

The dew heavy as milk on the grass, the bird ceaselessly denouncing the sleepwalking woman, the cloud sailing past with its ivy-tendrils dangling, the bright sun driving the cloud's golden engines, the bright sun drying the dew, evaporating the woman, a strain on the terrace and a white nightie soaking with dew, the butler strolling out and laying the table for breakfast, the woman waking up in bed to the denunciation of the bird. Then the wind suddenly drops, hiding in the oak-shadow on the lawn.

The last treadmill, with its inscription 'Be faithful to your God and King'. The strutted wood is grey with dust, the stained clothes wrap wax dummies, the old bell of Newgate prison accumulates silence in an adjacent corner.

High on the cornice are heads of revolutionary malefactors. Robespierre with the bandage still on his jaw and eyes lightly sleeping; his companion hanging bodiless by his hair looking down on his nothing with bolt-eyed terror; a third sunk very deep into the silence of his severed head, with crabbed lips and cheeks sucked hollow in petrified expectation fulfilled, and the severed edges of his neck clenched tight as a karate fist where its severance sprang away from the blade-blow.

The pallid light makes terrors of us too. Our cheeks are full of static blood like dabs of paint, our clothes are wrinkled and flimsy like withered skin, our lips speak with the writhing of drab earthworms.

It is not the crow-fruit heads that give me so much pain, or the vengeful inscription or the passing-bell poised for the next stroke or the underwater look of my fellow-visitors, but that when I watch us circulating through the exhibits, my gaze admires the restful stillness of the figure in the condemned cell; and when I study the rigid figure strapped for guillotining I relish small movements within my clothes too much, too sexily. Now the pangs of death send their ghosts into me. I leave the chamber of horrors with the back of my neck aching in a fiery ridge, my tongue filling my mouth so I cannot swallow.

The skins of giant toads sewn together to make warty maps.

As the explorer walked into the state apartments, the candle-flames bent towards him and followed as if they were pointing fingers.

He said that the grains of sand in that place weighed as heavy as dictionaries. He pointed to the palm of his left hand. 'If I laid such a stone as a grain of this sand on my hand, it would slip its way through in an instant.'

Will nobody believe the explorer? 'No, what I tell you is not exactly true, and you might not see exactly what I saw if you went there, but what I saw is truer than if it were told in another way by me, though not as untrue as if it were told by another person . . .'

'. . . that valley is the valley of the great earthworms, their worm-casts are the tumuli. There is a tree that fruits thin-walled floating globes into the air, and at certain seasons the air is thick with them, and thick with the squeals of the great earthworms that rear their heads out of the soil to plunge their snouts into the bubble fruit to drink . . .

'. . . the magicians in that land have a punishment, a curse, it is to salivate urine . . .'

That country . . . that valley . . . we enjoy the stories, but what if he brought such things here . . . ?

The ten stones lapped by the tide. The tide retreats. A crab emerges from the foot of each stone, parting the weed with an identical and simultaneous gesture. They march to the fresh stretch of salty sand at the centre of the stone circle. They mate, with the sound of typewriters. The tide is returning, they retreat to their caves. They have written their page on the sand, as a pack of cards writes its game on the baize table. The tide is coming like hands to gather up the writing.

She chances on the inscribed sand, leans over the waist-high boulder. She understands the script. The clouds stand still.

Now the horses come up to her in the meadow. She selects the stallion she needs and rides it into the wood. The stallion becomes her lover, they talk in words together. She is the lover of the animals. She has read Faust's book without losing her soul.

The cancer in her breast recedes, vanishes. It spoke the language of the animals, which is the language of the flesh. It is understood, and no longer exists as a cancer. She will learn the language of the stones, and if she does not, chalky arthritis will teach it to her by the squeaking of her joints. She will learn the language of the plants for otherwise her arterial blood will press into her brain and split its vivid syllables to glow for a moment there, and then die into derelict grey nervosities like the scabby tiles of city dwellings.

The language of men springs from the language of horses, and this heals the heart; in the wood, she lowers herself upon the tremendous kindly sweat of the horse.

The book is . . .

It is not a book it is a struggling bird I hold it by outstretched wings and it almost gets away but it is a book.

I begin to read and I hear words: a clay vase of water like a shrunken head to be held and not laid aside. I hold this vase and I wonder what will happen if I spill the water.

But the clay splits with the weight of water in it and the shards fall apart like pages and the water falls drenching my dress and shoes and spilling on the ground.

In the mud it makes a lengthening green mist which is grass with flowers in it, yellow primroses.

I pluck a primrose and another until I have gathered a bunch which opens in pages which read: orgasm reaped me.

But the yellow turns grey with the too many letters melting in it and the grey shrinks into its shell which I hold like a coiled paving-stone peeling with lichen. It is too heavy for me and I lay it on the ground when it splits with a great bass cry and odours of meat come from the spilt drapery, the hats, buttons and ribbons which dry on the dusty ground in the strong sun.

I am shrinking down into them smaller and smaller until I am a full stop on the garish page and I stare straight up into the sun with my eye which is drying into the paper but before it blinds I see a black spot answering my own nature on the sun's disc.

The sun spot grows larger and its plumes ripple like pages too bright to read but it is bending down and reading me. It is more colours than I can count, carrying all the jewels and all the minerals on its wings and I am clasping the leather of the book tight shut breathing as if I have been running hard and in the book I feel the pumping of my excited heart.

The white stream bumping over the rock looks like a man in a fluttering nightie trying to run into the rock. He resembles one who hears the rustling of the sun's feathers, he wishes to escape but there is no escape. The small stones of the shingle turned over by the tide look both woven and grainy, like tweed.

The sun drops, the beach is full of flexible shadows like flapping bibles, and laggard ones, looking as if they were cut out of soft lead.

The wind rises. The wooded hill swells. The sea is a promenade of grey stones for the wind, I see the great footsteps, I see the chorus porticoes open in it, the whistling caverns that fry white and close, the galloping chiffon spectres. Then the wind drops and the night bell raddled with stars drops over the world. I imagine another world through the pulsating doors. Then the white clapper-end painted like a moon swings slowly overhead and I hold my ears ready for the blow on the far rim which will split the sky into always light. I leave the beach. The little white shadow of the man is still running into the rock, as if it took very many years to penetrate even its outermost layer.

She comes like a seashell without a skin, like warm mud that moves in sections.

She comes like a tree-frog clambering towards some great fruit, niddip, niddip.

A small acrobat lives inside the flower. The canopy blooms.

Her blouse comes off like the clean paging of newly bought notebooks, there is a smell of fresh bread and a clean active animal with strong teats inside.

She has an underground belfry tolling the bushes, which shakes the ground.

It is full of shivering bats that fly out and return.

Her knickers come off like opening party invitations and between her legs pigeons are laying eggs without shells.

I have lost dread there longer than a man reasonably may, I believe I knew white lids sledding over mossy wells, shearing prisms and silk splitting for me to walk into a red room and inspect the portraits.

She wears the long series of wonder awakening dresses, the fishskin dress, the seamless dress of pearl with the constellations slashed into a dark lining, open it and you see the night sky. Each night of the year she is different.

She plucks a narcissus and the underworld opens in the water-meadows. The three girls have been playing in the water. Their blue dresses are wet and sparkle as they run. The sun is warm. An old woman sits in a cave. She sits just out of sight.

Teresa plucks a narcissus and the ground opens. The turf